Punching the V-Card

by Leta Blake

Other Books by Leta Blake

'90s Coming of Age Series
Pictures of You
You Are Not Me
Only You

Winter Holidays

North's Pole

The Mr. Christmas Series
Mr. Frosty Pants
Mr. Naughty List
Mr. Jingle Bells

A Boy for All Seasons
My December Daddy

Fantasy

Any Given Lifetime

Reimagined Fairy Tales

Flight
Levity

Paranormal & Shifters

Angel Undone
Omega Mine

Horror

Raise Up Heart

Omegaverse

Heat of Love Series
White Heat
Slow Heat
Alpha Heat
Slow Birth
Bitter Heat

For Sale Series
Heat for Sale
Bully for Sale

Audiobooks
letablake.com/audiobooks

Discover more about the author online

Leta Blake
letablake.com

Gay Romance Newsletter

Leta's newsletter will keep you up to date on her latest releases and news from the world of M/M romance. Join the mailing list today.

Leta Blake on Patreon

Become part of Leta Blake's Patreon community in order to access exclusive content, deleted scenes, extras, bonus stories, rewards, prizes, interviews, and more. www.patreon.com/letablake

Acknowledgements

Thank you to the following:

Daniela and Gwen for beta reading and discussing stuttering with me. My parents who have always supported and loved me. Brian & Cecily who believe and trust in me. All the wonderful members of my Patreon who inspire, support, and advise me. Sue Laybourn for the detailed editing work. Keira Andrews for editing, handholding, and our long-lasting friendship. Kim V for her loving friendship and hours of listening.

Most of all, thank you to my readers for making all the hard work worthwhile.

THURSDAY

Chapter One

DEVON WATERS' PALMS were sweaty as he steered his car into his parents' mountain driveway. His beloved blue 2015 Ford Taurus, paid for with his own hard-earned tips from waiting tables at O'Charley's, had performed well on the wet, stormy drive home from college. Even so, his stomach had been in knots the entire way, and not because of the weather.

He hadn't been this nervous since he'd come out to his folks at the end of his freshman year of college. That'd gone well, so there was every reason to hope this weekend would go well, too, right? And given that he was pretty well-practiced at all the activities he'd be pursuing over the next four days of his fall break, he didn't know what he was so anxious about.

As he pulled into his dad's usual spot in the two-car garage, since his folks were both out of town on work-related trips, his stomach flipped again. The presence of a yellow 1986 Camaro parked in their mother's car's usual place reminded him of exactly why he was so anxious. His younger sister Hope *and* her best friend, the singular, scrumptious (Devon's mother's description), and virginal Carl Pink had beaten him home.

Carl wasn't an unfamiliar presence at the house. Carl had been Hope's best friend all through high school, but it wasn't as if Devon *really* knew him. Ignoring his sister and her friends was basically in his job description as an older brother.

Devon *did* know peaches-and-cream Carl was called Pinky amongst his friends, both because of his last name *and* his delicate appearance. Not that Carl had a ton of friends, because despite being freakishly good-looking with swooping blond hair and such pale, frosty-blue eyes, Carl had one giant strike against him—he was also entirely out and proud. In Appalachian high schools like the one they'd all attended, being an out queer kid didn't bode well for popularity.

As far as Devon had heard, Carl's friends consisted of Hope and the four members of Carl's band, which was called, ridiculously, Pinky and The One Eyes. The euphemism was clear and, in Devon's opinion, immature. Though he'd heard (once again from Hope, and she was clearly biased) they were fantastic. *And* also breaking up.

Because said preternaturally beautiful Carl Pink was leaving town and his bandmates behind after Christmas. For good.

Hope said Carl was heading across the country to Los

Angeles to try to break into the music business on his own. Devon might have thought it was a bad idea, and he might even have worried for the kid out of sheer human decency, but there was no need. Carl was an only child, his folks were both rich and permissive, and, according to Hope, one thousand percent accepting of Carl's homosexuality and even more supportive of Carl's career aspirations. So, Devon suspected the fine-boned, pretty boy wouldn't be roughing it all that much out there in the land of honey and gold.

But the move *was* the reason Carl's Camaro was parked in Devon's parents' garage. And it was also the reason Devon's heart was thumping like crazy and his blood now rushed in his ears like a freight train.

It was stupid to be this frazzled, because he was supposed to be the jaded, experienced, unflappable older guy this weekend, wasn't he? That was his mission and the whole reason he was here. Yet his hands were shaking as he put the car in park and turned the ignition off. He'd always found Carl so beautiful that the idea of touching him was thrilling, but the circumstances around said potential touches were utterly nerve-wracking.

Devon sat in his car a minute longer, listening to the rain on the garage roof and trying to figure out just how this was going to go. But he didn't get anywhere with his thoughts before the door into the house was thrown open and Hope came bursting through to the garage, smiling and flushed, her brown eyes sparkling.

"Devon, you dumbass, get inside! I have to leave soon and I want to get you guys settled."

Settled. What did that even mean, given what was happening?

Devon waved at her and then reached into the back seat to get his duffle. He'd brought everything with him that he'd need, just like Hope had instructed, but he ran through a checklist in his head again, just to be sure. It wasn't a very long list, after all. Just three items. They weren't going to be doing anything complicated. And not that he'd had much to do with the planning of this weekend either. That had been all Hope and Carl. He'd mainly just been saddled with consenting.

Which he was beginning to doubt the sanity of.

It wasn't like he was hard up. He had options.

"Devon! Seriously! Hurry!"

Devon thought whoever it was who'd claimed oldest children were natural leaders and youngest children natural followers was cracked. How else to explain him and Hope? She was the little boss and he'd always ended up following her orders—even when it went against his better judgment.

One of his earliest memories of big-brotherdom came from when they were three and six. Hope had ordered him to climb the shelves in the pantry to get the hidden cookies, promising to share them with him if he did. But instead of splitting cookies with Hope, when the board of the shelf broke he'd split his head. He still had a scar from that, and it should have served as a warning to never let Hope talk him into anything rash.

But it didn't work out that way, since only thirty-eight annoying texts and four infuriating Skype calls had managed to convince Devon to cave and agree to this stupid plan.

As Devon climbed out of the car, his knees felt like jelly and his pulse beat wildly. Hope rushed over to take hold of his arm, dragging him toward the doorway leading into the kitchen. "He's already nervous. Don't make him think you're reluctant or something. God, how insulting would that be?"

Carl Pink nervous? It seemed so unlikely given his past experience with Carl's cocky, self-assured smugness that he didn't even need Hope to propel him forward into the kitchen. He wanted to see Carl in this unusual state for himself.

The kitchen was the same as ever—clean, midsized, and dominated by the big wooden table to the right of the kitchen counters. The rain hit the window beside the table, and his mother's beloved incandescent bulbs glowed in the hanging lamps over the main bar-height counter. Everything was normal, except his parents weren't here to greet him, despite the homey scent of pot roast permeating the air. Plus, there was a spread of cookies, veggies, nuts, and fruit sitting on the counter, most of it artfully plated and covered with plastic wrap.

And then there was Carl. Sitting on one of the stools at the kitchen counter, he held an acoustic guitar. Devon swallowed hard, eyes catching on the blond hair shimmering over his forearms and wrists as he picked out notes. Devon had always had a thing for details like that on a guy. It made them human, real, and touchable. He'd never thought of Carl as entirely real before, what with his surreal beauty and cold manner.

"Hey," Devon greeted him, hoping to sound casual, but his throat felt tight.

Carl nodded, not even glancing at him. Barefoot in blue jeans and a plain white T-shirt showing off the pale, smooth column of his neck and the soft-looking skin of his arms, he noodled on, keeping his gaze focused out of the kitchen window. He seemed more interested in the rain and the gray landscape than in the guy enlisted to do him this *favor*, or whatever this was to him.

Carl's expression was distant and, if Devon was going to put a name to it, smug. He didn't appear nervous at all, in Devon's opinion, which threw into doubt all of Hope's assertions and the reliability of her communications in this entire mess.

Because unlike Devon, Carl was acting like this was the sort of thing he did so often he was bored out of his mind even considering the prospect of doing it again.

Never mind that Devon had been told that wasn't the case. That was the whole purpose behind his even being here.

Was it too much to ask for Carl to at least seem excited? Or something? Jesus.

"So, I made a roast in the crock pot," Hope said, motioning toward the counter. "And I was just putting all this stuff in the fridge for you guys to eat later. Also, there's chips and salsa in the pantry, and you can always order pizza." She beamed, a little wild and bright, like she was excited about what lay ahead for her brother and her best friend. More excited than Carl seemed, that was for sure. It was kind of weird.

"Um, thanks?" Devon watched as Hope ran a hand through her short, dark, unruly hair. He'd always heard that he and Hope could've been twins except for his facial hair, which he kept shaved, but a five-o'clock shadow always crept in. Otherwise, they both shared pale, smooth skin, chocolate-brown eyes, wide lips, and curly almost-black hair.

Devon knew he was fine-looking enough, but it was only when he took an objective gander at Hope that he could kind of see why so many girls (and a lot of guys) found him handsome. Inside, though, he felt like his body didn't quite fit his soul yet, like he was a puppy still growing into his ungainly paws.

According to his last boyfriend, Jay—a hot ginger

with an amazing laugh—because Devon did appear to be a full-grown man, he should step up and start acting like one, too. That expectation might have had something to do with why they'd broken up.

But what Jay had meant by *"step up and act like a grown man,"* Devon still didn't know. What was more grown-up than going to college, doing his best work, trying to be a good person, and holding down a job, too? Was it really more adult to go clubbing and bar-hopping every night, having fun but being responsible to no one else? Devon didn't think so. But he wasn't going to start thinking about Jay right now.

Instead, he was going to try to understand the weirdness coming out of his sister's mouth.

"So, you should be all set for food. Melanie will be here to pick me up any second. I'm going to stay at her place, but I can be back over here in a flash if there's a problem." This last was addressed to Carl who wasn't looking at her either, paying more attention to the placement of his fingers on the neck of his guitar and the rainy window than to either Devon or Hope.

Hope's phone buzzed and she picked it up from the counter. "Okay, that's Mel. Here, help me get all these fruit and veggie plates in the fridge."

"It's not a goddamn house party," Devon muttered as he helped her, passing the plates so she could arrange them inside. He flicked a glance toward Carl, who was making a pretty melody with the guitar but had as yet to even say hi.

"Are you sure he really wants to do this?" Devon whispered in Hope's ear as she shut the refrigerator door.

"Of course!" She punched his shoulder and laughed. "Don't be stupid."

Devon didn't see how that was a stupid question at all, but he just raked a sweaty hand through his hair as his stomach tightened. How were they even going to…

When Carl was so…

Ugh. Why had he ever agreed to this? He could still back out. There was no reason he couldn't have a normal fall break full of TV marathons and hardcore sleeping. He'd just have to tell Hope and Carl to forget it.

Devon grunted under the weight of the heavy, army-green duffle bag Hope thrust into his arms as he followed her toward the front door. "That's Carl's stuff. Take it up to your room."

Devon dropped the bag by the stairs in the front entryway. He'd do it later. If they did it at all. Because it was becoming more and more doubtful they would, as far as he was concerned, what with the way Carl was acting.

The guitar squawked as Carl's fingers slid over the neck, and then Devon heard a ringing *clunk* as the guitar was put down. Then came the slap of Carl's bare feet on the wood floor behind Devon as he too came to say goodbye to Hope. Opening the front door for his sister, Devon could see Melanie's red Honda sitting in the driveway through the misty, gray rain.

After waving toward the car, Hope went up on tiptoe to kiss his cheek as she grabbed her bulging overnight bag from beneath the coat rack by the door. "Be gentle," she whispered.

Devon flushed.

Sputtered.

But stayed silent, because what the fuck was he supposed to say to that? His cheeks heated, and he cleared his throat. Like he'd ever be rough? But Hope just rolled her eyes at him before he could say anything. Then she grabbed Carl in a big, dramatic hug. They clung to each other, like Carl was facing some terrible task, one so dreadful that he required the fortification of bear hugs to endure it, which set off even more alarm bells in Devon's brain. If that was how Carl felt, why did he want to do it? Devon didn't understand.

As the hug dragged on, Devon couldn't help but admire Carl's blond hair contrasting with Hope's dark curls. Carl's slim shoulders and sharp shoulder blades looked fragile under Hope's healthy grasp. With a blink, Devon realized Carl wasn't even as tall as Hope, who stood a full half-foot shorter than Devon's rangy six-two. He'd always known Carl was small for a guy, it'd been one of his attractions even—ethereal, finely sculpted, and spritely—but he seemed smaller than ever in her arms.

Carl pulled back and winked at her. "It's fine," he told her in his deep voice.

It always startled Devon how gravelly and rough Carl sounded, like he smoked a pack a day or deep-throated thick-dicked truckers for a living. It was the exact opposite of his appearance, and the contradiction had always put Devon's dick on alert. He'd sat through several very awkward family dinners with a half-chub because of Carl's sexy voice and elfin face. And, okay, if he were honest, those evenings of unwanted attraction had fed into his eventual agreement to participate in this weekend's planned activities.

"Seriously, it's all good," Carl said. Hope looked like she might cry, which was just plain weird since, as far as Devon could tell, this had been all her idea. Carl kissed her forehead. "I'm fine. Go. Have fun with Melanie."

"Okay," Hope agreed and then shot Devon a sharp glance as if he'd done something wrong. He shook his head but didn't get to ask what the hell that was about because she turned, hiked her overnight bag onto her shoulder, and ran out into the rain. Her dark curls tightened into frizz as she darted between drops and climbed into her friend's car.

"That's all done, then," Carl said as they watched the red Honda back out of the drive and pull away. "That was the hard part." He cleared his throat. "Right?"

Devon had no idea what Carl was talking about but the slight rise at the end of the word *right* was the first time he'd ever heard Carl sound even close to uncertain about anything at all and so he said, "Right," like he even had a clue.

Carl nodded, stepped forward to take the front door out of Devon's hands, and shut it.

The autumnal gloom of the front hall swallowed any hope of reading Carl's expression, as did his swoopy hair falling into his face as he ducked his head. "I brought condoms and lube. We'll do it in your room." He turned briskly as if he were going to head upstairs to Devon's room right now to get this all over with.

"Wait," Devon said, grabbing Carl's arm. It was small and wiry against his palm, and he couldn't resist squeezing a little.

"What?"

"We need to have a talk first."

Carl pulled his arm free, cleared his throat, and lifted his chin. The wan light from the square windows over the front door fell onto his face, highlighting his strange, pale eyes. "We'll get the first time over with. That way we can practice specifics the rest of the weekend."

"No, Carl. That's not what we're going to do."

Carl's jaw clenched, as if he wasn't accustomed to being told no. And given how spoiled he was as an only child, maybe he wasn't. "Yes, it is," he said.

Devon snorted. He knew if he were a normal guy he'd be on the same page as Carl right now, dragging him upstairs to get his clothes off and all the rest.

But he wasn't a normal guy, and he kind of thought that was part of why Hope and Carl had planned Carl's first time to be with him, wasn't it?

So, nope. That wasn't how this was going to happen.

The idea of taking a guy up to his bed and fucking him before they'd even had a chance to talk didn't appeal. He'd had enough hookups in college to know he just wasn't that kind of guy. And if they were going to do this, he wasn't going to compromise who he was and what he liked, for Carl, or anyone.

"Back to the kitchen. Now," Devon ordered, trying to take charge. He was the older of the two of them, the more experienced, wasn't he? Who did Carl think he was trying to take control of when and how they were going to fuck? "We're talking this out whether you like it or not."

"Uh-uh. No," Carl said.

He sounded serious, like there was no way in hell he was going to back down. And Devon didn't know why. What in the hell was going on? He tilted his head, trying to get a better bead on the situation.

"We aren't going to talk about it." Carl's silver eyes gleamed in the low light. "Let's just get this done, all right? I know you want to fuck me." He lifted his sharp chin in a seductive way and gave Devon an obnoxiously confident stare. "Everyone does."

"Then why hasn't anyone done it yet?" Devon asked, putting his hands on his hips and lifting a brow. "Why'd you have to get Hope to beg me to do it?"

Carl sniffed. "There was no begging. I don't beg. If you don't want to do this, fine. We don't have to do it." He started to turn back to the kitchen, his back stiff and tense.

Devon rolled his eyes. "Stop being so dramatic. That's not what I said."

Carl stopped and turned, the light from the windows highlighting his eyes. He looked almost inhuman as he stood there, studying Devon like he didn't quite know what was making him tick, like he was trying to decide if Devon was made of flesh and blood. For that matter, was Carl? He was so cold he could've been made of snow. And Devon didn't intend to fuck a snow man.

"Look, just come in the kitchen with me to talk, all right? We're both here for a reason—"

"Exactly," Carl interrupted. "Let's get it done."

Devon dropped his voice a bit lower. Maybe Carl was scared, and this was how he dealt with his nerves. "Is it a crime to want to have a conversation first?"

"I really don't see the point," Carl said.

This wasn't how Devon had thought this *deflowering* would go. Which raised the question, how *had* he thought it would go? He didn't know anymore. Maybe he'd thought Carl would seem a little grateful? Or eager? Or something other than cold and alien, something other than *resentful.*

Did Carl not want this?

Devon's stomach twisted. He crossed one arm over his chest and rubbed the pad of his other thumb across his eyebrow. Silence filled the hall as dust-motes drifted around them almost like snow.

Thunder rolled.

They stood in the shadows of the hallway staring at each other. Confusion roiled inside Devon, along with the desire to walk back out to the garage, get into his Ford Taurus, and drive away. Where? He wasn't sure. Back to school, probably. Away from this, for sure.

Carl's tension collapsed, and his expression turned softer, his blond brows scrunching up. "Hey, it's okay," Carl said, his voice pitching lower, gentler than Devon had ever heard it. Grit in honey, a rough whisper.

Carl reached one thin hand into the space between them. The light from the windows fell on it, illuminating its steadiness and the bitten nails and callouses from guitar strings.

"What's okay?"

"This," Carl clarified. "This is okay."

"I'd feel better about it all if you'd talk to me," Devon said.

And if you weren't acting so damn weird.

Carl studied him again with his cool gaze. "Are you scared?"

Devon blew out a long breath and rubbed a hand through his hair. "Scared? Of you? Or of having sex with you? No. Definitely not afraid of either of those things. But am I weirded out? Absolutely."

Carl nodded and gestured for Devon to continue.

"Look, you've been friends with Hope for a long time, but I barely know you. I don't sleep with guys I don't know. I don't even understand why I agreed to do this." He flung a hand toward Carl. "And you! You're being creepy, honestly. It's like you're annoyed about this or something."

Carl shook his head, his blond hair cascading into his eyes again.

"I don't intend to fuck a guy who doesn't even want me. Or like me. Or *care* if I like him."

Carl groaned, and the dark sound curled around Devon's dick despite his misgivings and anxiety. "F-fuck. I'm doing this wrong. I kn-knew I would. I told her. *Fuck.*" He chewed on his plush bottom lip and then glanced up at Devon from beneath his hair. It was a pretty picture and made him look as innocent as he claimed to be. "Listen, I'm r-really bad with people. Like awful."

"Yeah? Why's that?"

"I don't know. B-b-because I switch off or s-something." He continued to stutter lightly and then licked his lips. He took a slow breath. "Will it help if I say I'm s-sorry?"

Devon blinked at him. "I think it'll help if we just go back to the kitchen. Start over. Slow things down. I'm not actually sure we should even do this."

Carl stepped forward then, his hand making contact with Devon's forearm. The touch was gentle and his fingers slid tenderly over his skin. Goosebumps rose all over Devon's body. Carl's brows bunched up again "The thing is I'm nervous and that makes me act…" He paused, and the next bit came out a little tense. "Like a dick."

"You don't seem nervous. You seem perfectly calm." Well, aside from the new stutters and the pressured sound to his speech. Since when did Carl have a stutter? Though maybe Devon vaguely recalled Hope mentioning once that Carl couldn't hang out because he was seeing his speech therapist. Devon hadn't really paid attention at the time, but it must have been for this.

"Well, I'm n-not."

"So you say. You also don't act like you care about me or what I want from all this. It's like you don't even like me," Devon admitted. "But if that were the case then I don't know why you'd want to have sex with me. Why fuck me if you don't even want to look at me?"

Carl's hand tightened on Devon's arm, stronger than he appeared. He tossed his hair off his forehead, gazing up at Devon with earnest, wide eyes rimmed with golden lashes that appeared almost glitter-dusted in the low light from the windows. "You're wrong." He again sounded tense, like each word cost him extra effort, so maybe he wasn't lying. "I l-like you. I've liked you a long time." His lips twisted a little lopsidedly. "I've l-l-liked you since before this grew in." He brushed his hand over Devon's cheek, touching his scratchy half-day's growth of beard. "I've liked you for y-years and years."

Devon scoffed, but didn't jerk away from Carl's calloused fingers skimming over his cheek. "You've only known Hope for like, I don't know, four years tops."

"Five this fall, actually." Carl swallowed, his sharp little Adam's apple bobbing, and went on, "And I've liked you every single one of th-th-those years."

Devon studied Carl's face, trying to see past the cool, collected expression. Was he even telling the truth? Devon couldn't read him. He just didn't know. "If that's the case, this is even weirder. You don't seem excited."

Carl's mouth broke into a full-fledged smile and he pulled his hand away. "Because I'm terrified that I'll…ss-screw this up."

"Yeah?"

"I do this thing when I'm scared. I g-go all…" Again that tense-sounding speech. "Cold and distant. Remote, my mom says. Ice prince, Hope says." Each phrase had a slight pause before it that added weight to the words.

Devon lifted a brow skeptically. Aside from his stutters, Carl didn't seem nervous. His hands didn't shake, his voice was scratchy but steady, and his eyes remained clear and intense.

Then Carl smirked. "Normally, I wouldn't even be t-t-talking right now. But for you I'm making an…an effort."

Huh. An effort? How strange. But if he wasn't lying, then maybe he did like Devon, and maybe he did want to have sex with him this weekend. Maybe.

Devon *wanted* to believe Carl and that was unnerving. Though, he supposed he should be able to believe the words of someone he was going to get naked and vulnerable with. "Normally, in a situation where you're nervous, how do you handle it?"

"Play guitar. Ignore everyone." Carl tilted his head again, considering. "Or I just get it over with. Whatever 'it' m-may be. It c-could be an audition, or a test, or something else that fr-freaks me out. Get it done, and I don't have to be scared anymore. In this case, it's sex. With you. And s-sex, period."

"So that's what you were doing before? When you basically demanded I go upstairs and fuck you now?"

Carl shrugged. Devon took that as a yes.

"Well," Devon said as gently as possible. "This isn't

the sort of thing you should 'just get over with.' It should be special."

"I know."

Devon frowned again. "And I don't sleep with guys who don't like me."

"But I *like* you, Devon, enough that b-being with you w-would be special to me," Carl said, and for the first time there was a hint of a kind of throaty desperation he'd never imagined hearing from him. It made Devon's nipples harden and his cock throb in expectation. "Please understand me. You have to be the one to do this for me."

"Whatever happened to, 'I don't beg' and 'We don't have to do this'?" Devon asked, lifting a brow. He knew he shouldn't tease, but he couldn't help it. He'd never seen Carl Pink even a little bit undone. And maybe, just maybe that had been a huge incentive behind him saying yes to this entire sordid plan.

Carl pressed his lips together in a firm line and then he stepped closer, close enough that Devon would only have to bend his head and lift Carl's chin to plant a kiss on his plump lips.

When he spoke again, his deep voice teased Devon's cock, and Devon didn't harbor any worry that Carl would be able to arouse him enough to perform. "L-look," Carl said quietly, so that Devon did have to bend his head to hear him better. "Isn't it enough that I've t-told you how much I like you? Even though confessing it sort of makes me want to th-throw up?" He looked up at Devon. "What more do you want from me?"

"An honest conversation."

"I'm being honest."

"I know, but before we have sex, we need to *really* talk. Set boundaries. Expectations. Discuss likes, dislikes, fantasies, fears. All of that."

Carl wrinkled his perfect little nose. "Do we though?" He slid his hands over Devon's arms seductively and pressed into his space. "I mean, if we just got it out of the way, we c-could relax and enjoy the rest of the weekend."

"If you like me, Carl, then you'll care what I want too."

Carl chewed on his lip again, moving in so, so close that Devon could feel the heat of his body, the sweetness of his breath filling the space between their mouths. "I care what you want. But I think it's cruel to make me wait when I've wanted you for…" Another pause. "For five years."

Devon choked on a laugh. "That's ridiculous."

The claim didn't compute. Every time he'd seen Carl, he'd been silent and stuck-up, ignoring Devon at best, and snubbing him at worst. Given how Carl had treated him in the past, Devon still didn't understand why he'd even agreed to this entire thing.

Hope had some kind of evil powers of persuasion.

Well, and there'd been the implicit promise of seeing Carl Pink *actually* flushed pink, trembling with want, and falling apart as he came undone. For Devon. There'd been that, too. And that image had been a huge draw. But what if Carl orgasmed in grim silence, all rigid and frozen? What then?

Devon's mind rebelled at that, ticking over into the planning phase: how to best tear down Carl's icy exterior until it disappeared. How to undo Carl Pink. He felt sure he could do it. But it would be on *his* terms, not Carl's. At least not Carl's *"get it over with"* terms. Maybe some of his other terms, depending on what they were, and what he wanted. Which was the entire point. They needed to have a conversation. And not this one about Carl crushing on Devon ever since he'd met him, despite every appearance to the contrary.

But Carl said he shut off when he was nervous, grew cold. Maybe he was telling the truth. Maybe he'd had crushed on Devon the entire time and that was why he'd seemed so stand-offish?

"What's the worst that could happen if we talk?"

"I'll like you more."

Devon rolled his eyes and snorted.

"See? You l-laughed," Carl said, still calm despite what should have been hurt-laced words. "I sh-shouldn't have told you that."

Devon sighed. Why was Carl so confusing? He put his hand on one of Carl's, which still rested on his arm, and tugged it off. "It's not that you shouldn't have said it, I guess I just don't believe it. I mean you can't like me all that much when you don't even know me."

Carl shrugged. "Fine, I can g-get to know you if it makes you h-happy."

That at least was in the direction Devon wanted to go, but did Carl have to sound so put out by it? Though perhaps it was the surprise stutter that Devon had never heard before—because Carl had so rarely talked before—that made him sound impatient.

"And would it really make *you* happy to just go upstairs to 'get it over with'? Would that really be what you want from me? Someone you claim to like? I don't understand that."

Carl looked at the floor and took a step back. "I know you don't have feelings for me, so I thought it would be less awkward for you, for us both, if we just did it. Th-that way I don't get confused."

"Confused about what?"

"About y-you liking me back." Carl stepped even farther back. Devon could see his pale eyes darken with shadows.

Devon furrowed his brow. "I don't understand."

"Sorry. Let me be clear. If we talk, and you laugh, and we get to know each other, I'll like you even more, but it can't m-mean anything."

"Right. You're leaving. I get it. But it's not like I'm going to fall in love with you."

"Exactly."

Devon blinked. "You are so hard to follow."

"And you're ob-obtuse."

Devon huffed. "See? That's not something you say to someone you like and who you're hoping will fuck you."

"I know, it's just…" Carl tossed his hair again. "I like you. You don't like me—"

"I don't *know* you!"

"—and if we talk, I'll like you more, and I'll start to h-hope. But, like you said, I'm leaving, and you probably wouldn't like me b-back anyway, because I'm a d-dick." He rolled his shoulders back and lifted his chin, a new sheen of iciness dropping over him. "If we just f-fuck each other, then I won't get confused. Get it now?"

Devon's heart twisted. He'd asked for clarity, and Carl had delivered, but he hadn't anticipated it being painful. He hadn't anticipated believing in Carl's crush, and yet, when he put it like that, Devon did.

"I get it."

"Besides," Carl said with a cool smirk. "I thought you'd want to f-fuck me right away. I mean, that's why you're even here, right? To get your dick wet."

Devon couldn't help but snort. "That just shows how little you know me."

"I'm figuring that out." Carl took Devon's hand into his own, the callouses on his fingers rough. "I do care what you want, Devon. I'm s-sorry I didn't act like I did at first. I understand now. It's important to you that we know each other before we have sex. So, h-horrible hope be damned—the emotion, not your sister—let's do this." He smiled, and it was the first real smile Devon had seen from him.

Between Carl's pink lips and cheeks, Devon had to admit that the nickname Pinky was apt. He wondered what else was that same color pink—his nipples? His cock? He supposed that by the end of the night he'd know for sure, if Carl had his way.

Carl tugged Devon gently toward the kitchen. "I want to do whatever it takes for you to be w-willing to do this for me."

As Devon followed, for the first time since he'd walked into the house, he felt like he might not have made the worst mistake ever in agreeing to relieve Carl Pink of his burdensome virginity.

Chapter Two

"I'VE BEEN WITH guys. I'm usually into topping, but I've bottomed, just so you know. I mean, if you want to try it both ways."

They sat at the kitchen table, the window pattering with rain. Carl was lounging in the chair next to Devon, the neck of his T-shirt stretched a little, exposing the tops of his collarbones. For his part, Devon had a pen and a yellow pad he'd grabbed out of a drawer in the kitchen, and he was clicking the pen again and again, ready to start a list.

"So we're doing this then?" Carl asked, his eyes brightening and his face lighting up. His stuttering had come and gone as they'd talked, but Devon hadn't asked about it. Carl seemed to steadfastly ignore it, and so would he. For now.

"Probably. I mean, it's why we're both here, and I guess if we can talk it over and agree to some kind of plan, then, yeah, we're going to have sex like you want."

Carl laughed and shook his head.

"What?"

"Nothing."

"No, tell me."

"I know you're not big on hookups like some guys, but when you were b-balking earlier, I got n-nervous that maybe you won't do it unless you're in love or something."

"Would that be so wrong?" Devon was sincerely curious.

Carl shook his head, suddenly looking shy.

Progress, Devon thought.

"Nah." Carl turned his attention to his fingers and started to pick at a nail. "That's kind of why I'm a v-virgin. I mean, I've had my share of offers, but I didn't want it to be j-just anyone."

Devon felt a knot inside him untangle a little. He only half-believed that Carl had a crush on him, but it made him feel better that he wasn't just an available cock for Carl to use to punch his v-card. Devon didn't want to be *"just anyone."*

"What was your first time like?" Carl asked, raising his head with sudden interest. "Or is that too personal?"

Devon shrugged. "I think what we're planning to do is really personal, and I wouldn't want to do it with someone I wasn't willing to talk to about things like that."

Carl's eyes seemed to glow in the gray light from the window, like silver or moons.

"My first time was with a guy I thought I was in love with," Devon said with a self-deprecating sneer. "I was eighteen and it was the third week of my first semester at college. I'd never felt that way about a guy before. Sure, I'd been attracted, but this was new. Buzzy, you know? Thought I'd die every time he even looked at me."

"Was he that handsome?" Carl murmured, going back to his nails.

"He was a soccer player. Amazing body."

"Great butt?"

"Oh, yeah."

"N-nothing like me then." He picked at the skin by his thumbnail.

"Your butt's fine."

The corner of Carl's mouth seemed to droop a little and Devon quickly course-corrected. Carl might've been a smug little jerk, but he had feelings and insecurities like anyone. "I mean, your ass is great. It's hard to tell in those jeans since you wear them all baggy, but your ass is pretty cute, from what I can see."

Carl didn't look at him, continuing to pick at his thumb. Devon made a note that if he saw Carl's naked ass, and it seemed very likely he would and soon, he'd definitely tell him good things about it, because even if it was flat, or small, it was Carl's and that meant it was a pretty sexy ass.

"What was his name?" Carl murmured. "Your first."

"Beckett. He said all the right things and kept me around for a few weeks after I gave it up to him, but then he was done." Devon rolled his eyes. He wished that didn't still sting. "Since then I've had other boyfriends, but only one kind of serious one named Jay. And, for the record, I don't just sleep with guys I'm in love with, but it's better when I care about them, and I won't do it at all if I don't at least like them a little. I've been propositioned by men I didn't know, and even one guy I actively didn't like, and I'm just not interested." Remembering Jay, he added, "I've been told that makes me prudish, but I don't really give a fuck what people think, I guess."

"Fuck whoever said that to you. For real."

"And, for full disclosure, I've had some friends with benefits arrangements, too. Low commitment, but I still know them well. That's it."

"That's what I didn't want," Carl said. "Uh, not what happened with your first, but the other stuff. I didn't want to be with a stranger, and I didn't want my first time to be with someone I just like as a friend."

Devon's stomach tightened oddly. He felt honored by that declaration and harbored doubt about it as well. "But in a way, that's exactly what this is: a friends-with-benefits-for-the-weekend sort of arrangement."

"To you, maybe, but not to me. If you don't think I know you, then you haven't been paying attention. Because I know *a lot* about you. All the important things."

Devon scoffed.

"It's true. I know you're kind, and that you love your sister. I know you'll be g-gentle even if it means n-nothing to you."

"It doesn't mean nothing to me."

"But it doesn't mean as much to you as it does to me." Carl smiled, and it touched the corners of his eyes. Devon's heart fluttered. "I get it. But don't d-downplay my feelings just because you d-don't share them."

Devon wanted to say it wasn't that he didn't share them, but that he didn't see any evidence of these feelings in Carl's behavior, just from his mouth.

Devon said, "You don't have to flatter me to get laid. I mean, to be honest, you're not exactly—"

"Your type?"

"What? No." Devon clicked the pen and drew a star on the edge of the paper. His heartbeat went all wonky. "You're pretty much exactly my type except for how you've always acted like a little stuck-up shit around me." He met Carl's eyes again. "I was going to say you're not exactly hard to want, so you don't have to make stuff up."

"I wasn't making anything up, but okay, if you don't want to hear it, I won't say it again." Carl's mouth turned down slightly at the corners, and the blue of his eyes seemed to crystalize a little more.

Oh.

Maybe Carl was a subtle guy and reading him took more effort Devon was used to. The idea that he wasn't devoid of true emotion was reassuring. Devon cleared his throat, deciding that if all this was going to happen, then he should take charge and act like he knew what he was doing.

He clicked the pen and declared, "First rule for the weekend: If we do fuck, we use condoms—no exceptions." He wrote *condoms* on the yellow pad.

"Condoms. No prob." Carl tapped his fingers on the table in a slow rhythm.

"Second rule for the weekend: we agree to boundaries ahead of time, and we don't cross them."

Tap, tap. "Sure."

Devon said, "Boundary number one: no, means no. Stop means stop."

"Of course. What else would it mean?"

"Some people like to play games where no doesn't mean no, and stop doesn't mean stop, but that should always be made clear in advance—"

"I know, Devon." Carl's lips curled up into a small grin. "I've watched porn. I've read about stuff."

Devon rolled his eyes. "I just want us both to be clear that everything we do is mutually consensual."

"I wouldn't want it any other way." Carl snatched the pen from his hand and pulled the yellow pad toward him. "Let's get started," he said, writing the words *THE PLAN* across the top of the pad.

"I've never been kissed, so I want to learn how," he said, writing *kissing* at the top. "I've never sucked cock, and I want to be good at it, so—" *cocksucking* appeared beneath kissing. "And reciprocation there would be great." He drew a two-way arrow beside it. "Fucking, obviously, topping and bottoming." He drew an up and down arrow. "Rimming. I've seen it in porn. Not sure how I feel about it? Is it gross?"

"It feels amazing, but if you don't want to do it—"

"Rimming," he said, writing it also with a two-way arrow and a question mark.

"Put down fingering," Devon said. "You'll want to get good at that. If you can finger a guy well, then he'll be eager for whatever else you want to do with him, I promise. And you'll want to experience it yourself too."

Fingering went on the list.

"And then I guess I want to put it all together." Carl drew a circle around it all. "Do you have any objections? Do you consent to teaching me all of this?"

"You're such a control freak," Devon said, pulling the pen away and adding at the bottom, *Lose control.* "That's the goal for the weekend. I want to see you lose it."

"All right," Carl said, and his voice was low and throaty. His pupils had gone wide and dark. It occurred to Devon that Carl hadn't stuttered even once since he'd taken hold of the pen. "Can we start now?"

"One more thing: nipple play. Guys either really like it or don't much care for it, but we should give it a go."

"Whatever you want to do to me is fine," Carl said. "If you want to lick the backs of my knees, I'll let you. I just want you to touch me, Devon."

Nipple play went on the list, as Devon's heart beat triple time and his cock thudded against his jeans.

"Never been kissed, huh?" he asked in a whisper.

Carl shook his head and leaned forward. "Kiss me."

Devon stood, the front of his jeans bulging with his arousal. Making the list and thinking of doing all those things with Carl until he came apart for real, until he lost this icy control, had turned him on.

"Not here." He took hold of Carl's calloused hand, the fingers fitting well in his own. "Upstairs. Where we can be comfortable."

Carl's jeans were also pushed out in the front, and he stood, letting Devon pull him toward the stairs. They stopped to grab Carl's bag. "I have supplies in there," he whispered.

"We won't need them quite yet," Devon replied.

Upstairs, Devon pushed the door of his bedroom shut behind them and locked it. He didn't know why. They were alone in the house, but the sound of the lock clicking in place made the situation real. He was in his bedroom, rain pouring on the roof, clacking against the big window that looked out into the forested back yard, and Carl Pink was pulling off his shirt and tossing it aside.

Devon's objection caught in his throat. He'd intended to start with fully clothed kissing, to get accustomed to the taste and smell of each other, to learn a little about how they interacted, but at the sight of Carl's white chest and pink nipples, and the blond fuzz trailing beneath his jeans, all words died.

Carl, eyes trained on Devon, shucked his jeans, too, so that he stood there in white boxer briefs alone, the crotch distended and wet with pre-cum already.

"Christ," Devon murmured, his own dick throbbing hard.

Carl lifted his arms in a shrugging motion, as if to say, "This is it, this is all I have." Devon swallowed hard.

"You don't have to get down to your underwear to learn to kiss," Devon said, tugging his own shirt over his head and unbuttoning his jeans to let some pressure off. "But I guess we can."

Carl grinned, and the electric shock of that smile hit Devon right in the solar plexus. His hands shook as he pushed his jeans down and off, and then the two of them sat in their underwear at the end of Devon's bed.

He'd jerked off so many nights in this bed, in this room, but he'd never kissed a guy on it, not even once.

In that way, Carl would be his first, too.

"So, uh," Devon said, realizing the problem with being mostly naked when he was trying to instruct a newbie on the art of kissing. There was skin everywhere and all of it just within reach. How was he supposed to do this without just shoving Carl onto his back and humping against his leg?

Carl shifted beside him, obviously uncomfortable, gripping his own dick and squeezing it through his underwear. Devon watched as the wet patch grew bigger, and his own cock flexed, releasing a small pulse of pre-cum, too.

"This okay?" Carl asked, as he rubbed at his cock and gazed at Devon. His throat was already pink, and his chest was splotchy with a rosy color. His nipples were raised and hard, and Devon nearly swallowed his tongue when Carl pushed aside the opening in his underwear and pulled his cock out. It was pink, very pink, and the tip was shiny and glistening. Pinky's one eye was leaking and making quite a sexy mess.

Devon licked his lips, clenched his hands into the comforter, and tried to get his head straight. Kissing. He was supposed to teach Carl about kissing. Fuck.

"Um, we should get dressed again," Devon gritted out. "Otherwise, I don't think this is going to go slow after all."

"I'm okay with that."

Of course Carl was okay with that! It was what he'd wanted from the beginning!

Devon reached out with a shaking hand, and said, "First, when you're going to kiss someone, you should—" His eyes flicked to where Carl was stroking himself, the head of his cock peeking through the opening in his fist, and disappearing again. "Do you want to come first? So we can concentrate?"

Carl shook his head. "Kiss me. Just show me."

Devon touched Carl's cheek, surprised by the beginning of stubble on the otherwise smooth skin, and leaned in. Carl's breath was hot on his lips. Devon felt the jerky movement of Carl's arm as he continued to stroke himself. He could see how this would end, and he knew if he wanted to have any pretense of control for the rest of the weekend, he should make them both get dressed again, calm down, and take this slower—one step at a time, the way he'd imagined it would be.

But there was no ending it now. He was too aroused, and Carl was too turned-on. They were unstoppable.

Their lips touched and Carl gasped.

Then Devon was the one gasping as Carl pushed hard against his shoulders and shoved him onto the mattress, crawling on top of him and kissing his mouth messily, roughly, and with no art whatsoever. His desperation was so intense that Devon gave into it. He let Carl take possession of his mouth, and, wrapping his arms around him, he slid his hands to cup Carl's rutting ass.

Because *of course* Carl was thrusting against Devon already, his bare cock sliding over Devon's stomach and catching in the fabric of Devon's boxer briefs. Carl groaned and Devon slipped his hands beneath the waistband of Carl's underwear, letting his fingers glide into Carl's crack and slide over his asshole.

Carl bucked hard. He yelled into Devon's mouth, a rough sound that shook them both, as he jerked and twitched, releasing bursts of hot cum all over Devon's stomach and chest.

"Oh fuck," Carl cried, tossing his head back, and his throat staining bright red. "Fucking fuck!"

Devon gulped, staring up at Carl Pink, undone already and out of control. He guessed that was one thing he could cross off his list, then? He'd thought it would be harder than simply letting Carl rub off on him while inexpertly attacking his mouth. He'd thought it would be the hardest thing on the list to achieve.

But it hadn't been.

It'd been the easiest.

All it took to make Carl Pink get real was touching Devon Waters. Maybe the kid hadn't be exaggerating about his crush after all.

Wow.

Chapter Three

CARL TWITCHED AGAINST Devon and whimpered into his mouth again, still moving on top of him, making unearthly noises. Devon ran soothing hands up his back, easing him and trying not to push his own aching dick up for relief.

"S-s-sorry," Carl stuttered, shivering and jerking from aftershocks. "That's…not what you w-wanted, is it? I'm…I'm sorry."

"It was fine," Devon said, though his mouth was a little raw-feeling from the clash of lips, teeth, and tongue he'd been subjected to while Carl had succumbed to ecstasy. "You were fine."

"Did you…" Carl pushed down with his hips, gazing at Devon with big, shocked eyes. Once again, Devon was taken aback by the emotion he saw in the typically emotion-devoid depths of crystal blue. "You didn't! Oh, man, how embarrassing."

Devon couldn't hold back a small laugh. "Don't be embarrassed, a few more seconds and I would have come, too."

"How can I help you?" Carl sat back on his heels, between Devon's legs, and looked him over. "You're...wow. That's my cum on you," he said, dazedly. "I don't know what to do. Should I apologize or l-l-lick it up?"

Devon's hips bucked at those words and before he could make up his mind, Carl was leaning over him, tongue out, to clean up his mess.

Devon couldn't even remember the last guy he'd been with who'd done something like that; he'd never have expected it from a complete innocent. Which, now that he'd experienced Carl's kiss, he had no doubt Carl was a virgin, but holy shit he was a *kinky* little virgin.

Or former virgin.

By modern standards, it was fair to say he'd had sex with Carl now. He was *deflowered* and Devon's job was done, though he figured Carl would argue the point. Something told Devon that Carl wouldn't be satisfied until he'd experienced anal at least once.

Carl's tongue tickled over Devon's ribcage and down to his belly button. He lapped up most of the cum, and then rose with glowing cheeks and eyes, and stared at Devon. "Now what?" he asked. "I can try a hand job, but I've never given one to anyone but m-myself, so I can't p-promise you'll like it."

"I'll like it," Devon said, shoving his underwear around his hips so that his cock and balls were free. "But you don't have to if you don't want to. We're supposed to be kissing."

"I don't think I was very good at that," Carl said, and then reached forward, eyes avid, as he traced a finger over Devon's dick. "Wow, that's going to go inside me? You're bigger than I thought you'd be."

Devon coughed. He wasn't all *that* big, not compared to the guys in porn, which Carl had claimed to watch, and so he wasn't sure what to make of the idea that Carl had thought he'd be smaller. After all, Carl himself was a little longer than Devon, and maybe a bit thicker.

"It's pretty," Carl said, sliding a finger over the head. "You're cut."

Devon nodded.

Carl peered at his own cock and touched the skin bunched around the pink, still-turgid head. "I'm not." He glanced up at Devon. "Do you care about that?"

These small glimpses of insecurity were wild, given how icy Carl had been when Devon had first arrived, but this was what he'd wanted, wasn't it? To see the real Carl Pink behind the coldness, and to break through that ice. But he hadn't imagined it'd be like this. He'd thought Carl would need to be cracked open, and instead Carl just took charge and broke his own shell apart to show Devon these glimpses of his raw, beating heart.

"I like cut and uncut cocks," Devon said. "They're

nice both ways."

"Can I suck it?"

Devon gasped. Part of him wanted to say, "Not yet," but another part of him—the part that hadn't come yet and was aching to unload, and preferably into something hot and wet—wanted to beg him to open his mouth and take him inside. "Let's kiss a little first. If you use your teeth on my dick, the way you did on my mouth…"

Carl's cheeks flared, and he glanced to the side in embarrassment. "I knew I was messing it up, but I couldn't s-stop m-myself."

"It's fine," Devon said, lifting his arms. "C'mere and rest next to me. We can practice a little, and you can hold my cock."

"Hold it?"

"To start. Then jerk it. Then I'll let you make me come."

"Oh!" Carl gasped, and he was next to Devon and nestled against his side in a heartbeat. "I want to see you come. I've imagined it so many times. I used to get hard playing solos on my guitar because I'd pretend the guitar was you, and I was working to get you off."

"Wow." Devon chuckled. "I had no idea."

"I know. You barely knew I existed." Carl reached out and touched Devon's cheek the way Devon had touched his earlier. "Now kiss me. I promise I can be a fast learner."

"I knew you existed, but—" Devon cut himself off, and leaned forward to brush their lips together. "You can start soft like this." He kissed the plumpness of Carl's lower lip, and then his top lip, and sucked lightly. "Try that."

Carl did as instructed, and Devon melted a little. "That okay?" Carl asked.

"Yeah," Devon said, reaching up to wind his fingers into Carl's hair. "You can do this, too. It feels sexy, and intimate, to run your fingers through the other person's hair." Carl shivered against him. "And the other person likes it, usually. Just don't pull. At first."

Carl kissed Devon's mouth again, and his hips started twitching against Devon's with a renewed hard-on. They practiced, fingers in each other's hair, touching lips together, and barely adding tongue, for a long time, until Carl was panting and humping harder, well on his way to a second orgasm when Devon still hadn't had a first.

"That's good," Devon encouraged when Carl got adventurous and started mouthing around Devon's throat and jawline. "That's really good."

He took hold of Carl's hand and brought it to his stomach, which was a little sticky from where Carl had licked up his own jizz earlier. "I'm going to move your hand down now, all right? Do you want to hold my dick?"

Carl shivered against him, and nodded, breaking free

of Devon's fingers to slide his hand beneath Devon's belly button along his treasure trail.

"Hold up," Devon said, grabbing Carl's wrist before he could reach Devon's dick. "Let me put your hand on me, all right? Just this time. I want to show you how I like to be stroked."

Carl groaned and kissed Devon's earlobe, whispering, "Show me."

Devon grinned, and then with shaking hands positioned Carl's hand on his cock and helped him squeeze it just the right amount. "Much harder and it'll hurt, much softer and I won't be able to get off, and I'm pretty ready to come already."

"Fuck," Carl murmured, shifting up on his elbow to look at where he held Devon's dick in his palm. "Oh, my God, holy shit, I jerked off so many times thinking about your cock in my hand, pretending my dick was yours, and my orgasm was yours, and—"

"Jesus, Carl."

"You never knew," he supplied. "I know. I never wanted you to know, but then I was going to l–l–leave and I just...I didn't want to go out there as a v-virgin, and..." He stared at his hand moving over Devon's cock, guided by Devon's own grip, and he seemed mesmerized, and based on his cock digging into Devon's hip, totally aroused. "I had to do this with you. I just had to know what you were like." His eyes shifted up to Devon's face.

"I had to see you like this."

Devon's toes clenched and unclenched as the strokes rubbed him just the right way, and Carl's guitar callouses provided a tantalizing scrape against the sensitive ridge of his cockhead. "Why?" he gasped. "Why me?"

"You're hot," Carl said. "Obviously."

"Ungh," Devon groaned as his cock passed through Carl's flexing grip.

"And nice."

"Carl, I'm—"

"And you care about things, you care about being a good person—"

"I'm going to—"

Carl stroked harder and faster. "And as long as I've known you, as soon as I heard you were gay, I knew I wanted you to be the one to teach me how to make a man come."

"It's not hard—" Devon gasped. "I'm gonna—"

"No, you're not," Carl said, pulling away with a smirk, and holding Devon's hand back from grabbing his own cock to stroke, too. "Not yet."

"Fuck!" Devon shouted, his cock twitching, unfulfilled, and his balls aching as his hips bucked up hard, seeking that final push over. "What the fuck?" He groaned. "Why?"

Carl laughed. "Because I want to make you remember this first orgasm with me forever."

"What are you talking about?" Devon groaned.

"I want you to beg for it."

Devon huffed. "*You* beg for it."

"Me?"

"Beg for my cum."

"And if I don't?"

Devon squirmed. He was so out of his depth with this confusing kid, and his cock was about to explode, and he didn't know what to do, how to get off and still be in control (had he ever been in control?), or how to make Carl lose it again. "You don't want to taste it?"

"Taste your cum?" Carl asked with keen eyes. "Yes. Can I suck the tip? Just enough to get it in my mouth? Just to taste you."

"You'll suck it until I come," Devon said, trying to sound authoritative. Somehow, he just sounded confused because he'd thought they'd do blow jobs *after* they'd done kissing and hand jobs, and now he didn't know what was going on.

He did know Carl was already bending over and taking hold of Devon's cock at the base again and aiming the head of it toward his lips.

"No teeth. Like how I taught you on my mouth."

"Mm-hmm," Carl agreed, his lips descending toward the leaking crown of Devon's dick. "No teeth."

And then came sweet, wet, heat on his cockhead, and Carl's eager tongue trilling over his sensitive slit. "Fuck,"

Devon whimpered, trying to keep from hunching up and forcing his cock deeper into Carl's mouth. "I'm going to come fast, so—be ready."

Carl didn't try to suck on the entire head, or put any part of Devon's dick fully into his mouth, but he worked just the tip and slit with his tongue and lips, and Devon couldn't resist running his hand through Carl's hair as he teased him higher and higher.

His nipples tingled, and Devon tugged on them to try to hold back from coming, and then then his balls jerked up and his toes flexed and his legs started shaking. "I'm gonna—this time, I mean it," he gasped in warning. "I'm gonna—"

Carl opened his mouth and pressed Devon's cockhead inside against his tongue and jerked the base of Devon's dick up and down with his calloused fingers. The tension grew, coiled at the base of Devon's spine, grabbed hold of his deepest core, and then pumped out with a shattering ecstasy that left him gripping Carl's hair too hard and shouting as he convulsed on the bed.

Carl tried to catch it all, but there was soon a pool of cum around the base of Devon's cock, slick in his dark pubic hair, and more leaking from Carl's mouth. He pulled back, his lips red and his tongue sliding out to lick Devon's cum from his chin and upper lip.

"Fuck," Devon groaned, his limbs still trembling. "You're…"

"What?"

"You're demanding," he muttered between chattering teeth. "We were just supposed to kiss for now."

"I'm an only child," Carl said with an impish grin that made Devon's heart do weird things. "I always get what I want."

"And what do you want now?" Devon asked, panting.

"To kiss you some more," Carl said, his still-hard cock pushing against Devon's side as Carl settled back in and began to kiss Devon's mouth again, sharing the taste of Devon's cum on his tongue. "And after this, how about you teach me to rim?"

Devon groaned, his cock twitching with aftershocks, but he settled in to making out with Carl as he tried to calm his nerve endings. He needed to break out of the endorphin- and sex-induced haze he'd been in from the moment Carl had shucked his shirt. He needed to slow things down. Take control.

Ten minutes later, slick with spit, sweat, and more of Carl's cum, he found taking control was impossible. It seemed, with Carl, he was only capable of losing it.

Chapter Four

"ARE YOU SURE about this?" Carl asked, and it was the first time he'd sounded uncertain about anything they'd done since he'd taken his shirt off. "What if I'm not clean enough?"

Devon, from where he was kneeling on the floor with Carl's ass right in front of him, and his cock and balls, too, could see that Carl was plenty clean. He breathed against Carl's hole and grinned when Carl gasped, his sphincter twitching. "I'm sure you are, but if you'd rather I didn't, we could do something else. Like blow jobs. Or take a break."

They could both use a break. Carl had come twice now, and Devon only once, but they'd been kissing so long they both had stubble burn on their chins, and the weekend had just started. They should slow down. Devon should stop letting Carl take them off the rails like this. Devon was the more experienced one. He should call the shots, and he should declare it time to go eat something and chill—non-sexually—on the sofa for a while. Maybe talk. Maybe sleep.

But Carl's asshole was right there in front of him, and it was the prettiest shade of pink Devon had ever seen. There was barely any hair around it, and Carl had put himself into this very vulnerable position—ass on the edge of the mattress, holding his own legs open and back—and told Devon to eat his hole.

"It's c-clean?" Carl asked again.

"Yeah. It's as clean as any hole I've ever seen."

Carl grumbled. "Don't really want you talking about other guys' assholes while you're looking at m-mine."

Devon laughed and rubbed his light stubble against Carl's butt cheek and then pushed him wide open, breathing against the small, twitching ring of muscle that he now felt sure he'd push his dick past before midnight. He had a feeling there was no way Carl was waiting, and he'd already proven himself incapable of applying the brakes the way he should.

"That feels so weird," Carl said, and his gravelly voice sounded tight. "Lick it now."

Devon huffed. Of course Carl tried to take control just as he'd been about to introduce him to an all-new praise Jesus kind of moment. He decided to play Carl's game. "And if I don't?"

"Lick it," Carl ordered. "Now."

Devon groaned and leaned in, almost as if a force other than his own will compelled him. He licked the swirl of flesh and took pride in the way Carl jumped at the sensation.

"Fuck," Carl snarled. "Th-th…that's a lot."

"Do you want me to stop?"

Carl brought his legs even higher and muttered, "Don't you dare."

Devon went back to work. He started gingerly at first, slow and easy, and then grew more insistent as Carl's breathing went wonky and his legs trembled and the muscles in his thighs and butt jumped. "Oh, wow," Carl groaned, his voice all gritty and desperate. "That's so good."

"Mm-hmm," Devon said, licking the flexing sphincter. "Ever put anything in here?"

"Fingers. The tip of my razor handle—no blade attached, obviously, and just the tip."

"Horny boy."

"Fuck," Carl said as Devon drilled his opening with his tongue. "Are you g-gonna? With your tongue? In me?"

"You want me to?"

"P-p-p," Carl tried to get it out. "P-p—ugh, yes, do it."

Devon kissed Carl's butt cheeks, trembling sweetly on either side of his target, and then blew on Carl's tight balls before going back to his asshole, which was wet and twitching. "All right," he said with a laugh. "Here it comes. Sure you don't want to learn about blow jobs first?"

Carl growled, "Don't make me give you payback for dragging this out."

"What if this is my payback for that orgasm denial you inflicted on me earlier?"

"You wanted it."

"Maybe you want it now."

"Fucking hell, D-D-Devon. P-please."

The stuttering was fascinating, and Devon made a note to ask about it later, but right now he had a very sweet hole in front of him and Carl Pink begging him to rail it with his tongue, and even though none of this was how he'd imagined this weekend would go, he couldn't say he hated it.

In fact, he kind of thought it was amazing.

Like Carl's cry when Devon pushed his tongue into him, then pulled it out, only to jab it back inside. Carl's hole spasmed, and Devon had to work his tongue to get it fucking into him again.

"Oh my God," Carl crowed, and his balls drew up tight. His feet flexed, and Devon was pretty sure he knew before Carl did that he was going to come from this. "Oh fuck! Fuck! *Fuck!*" he screamed as he blew a load without touching his dick and with Devon's tongue still shoved into him.

"Oh, Jesus," he moaned as Devon fucked in and out, licking the rim of his asshole and kissing it as Carl trembled all over with aftershocks. "I…did—did—n't—Fuck, I had no idea. Fuck. *Fuck.*"

Devon kissed the pucker of his hole and then pulled away, standing up to gaze down at Carl. The comforter was a wreck where he'd bunched it in his fists, and from where they'd rolled around making out, and now it was gathered up beneath Carl in uncomfortable-looking hills, but he didn't seem to care. His body was flushed, his cock a glistening pink, his pubes soaked in his cum, and his nipples pert and red. He still held his legs back, and his hole glistened with spit. As Devon ran his eyes over Carl from head to twitching hole, he ached to push his cock inside.

But no.

Not yet.

Devon hadn't even fingered him. He didn't have a condom ready. He was not going to fuck him. No way.

But he *was* going to come again.

Now. He needed it.

Devon stood at the end of the bed, cock aimed at Carl's chest, and jerked slowly, steadily, staring into his brilliantly blue eyes, watching him and being watched.

"You going to come for me?" Carl asked, all low and deep, with his chest still heaving. "I want it on me. All over me. Paint me."

How had he learned to be so dirty? Such a fresh little innocent and yet so firm and filthy in what he wanted.

So shameless.

"Suck it," Devon demanded, a sudden need to get Carl's mouth on his cock again surging through him.

"No," Carl said, shaking his head. "Come on me, or don't come at all."

Where did he get these things? This natural dominance? Devon had no idea, but before he could process what to say in response, his balls seized up, his eyes rolled back, and he was shooting onto Carl's body as Carl arched to catch it. He looked ecstatic as Devon's cum splattered his chest and stomach, as it painted one of his nipples and splashed over his neck. Devon's knees buckled from the force of his orgasm.

"That's it," Carl said reaching for Devon and pulling him down on top of him. "You're a good boy," he said, stroking his back. "A good teacher. A very good asslicker."

"Are you sure you've never done this before?" Devon gasped, quaking against him as they smeared their cum between their sweaty bodies. "Who taught you to talk like that?"

"I don't know. I just want to say these things to you. I like the look on your face. I like how you can't help but do what I tell you to do. What's that mean? Does it mean I'm an asshole?"

"Maybe. But I think you're a natural dom."

"Dom? Like those guys who hurt their lovers for fun?

No, I don't think I'd like that."

"I'm too tired right now to explain it," Devon muttered. "Later. After we rest."

"You're done for today?" Carl asked, sounding a little disappointed.

Devon chuckled. "I'm sure we're not through quite yet. But give me a minute. I'm exhausted."

As they lay together in bed, Carl held Devon close and sniffed at his hair with affection. "You smell good," he said. "And you're really hot when you come, did you know? You make this face that looks like your soul's about to leave your body."

"Shh."

"I'm giving you a compliment."

"You're hot too," Devon muttered. "But I'm trying to sleep."

"How am I hot?"

"Trying to sleep."

"But how?"

"Ugh, the way you turn all pink, and you're so bossy. It's hot."

Carl seemed satisfied by that because he patted Devon's hair and said, "Rest. Later, I'll have you fuck me."

"After dinner."

"Sure. And after blow jobs."

"We'll fuck tomorrow," Devon murmured, sleep tugging at him. "Blow jobs tonight."

"We'll see," Carl said. "We'll just see about that."

The next thing Devon saw was an ocean full of stars as sleep claimed him in delicious recovery.

Chapter Five

"A POT ROAST," Devon said, poking at the food. "She made us a pot roast. What the hell? Who does that?"

Carl sat across from him eating a salad and sipping water. He'd been pretty quiet since they'd woken from their nap. They were both freshly scrubbed from a shower that hadn't gotten sexy, which had surprised Devon until he'd heard the rumbling from Carl's tummy. Then he'd understood that he was just hungry for food and not dick.

"And why does it taste so weird," Devon said, frowning. "It's like meat, but not meat."

"It's tofu."

"Tofu?"

"Vegan."

"Why?" Devon boggled. "I mean, are you vegan?"

"No, but I told her that meat was a bad idea if we're going t-to…at least, that's what I read online. Wh-when I w-w—argh," he let out in frustration. "It's what I read online," he finished in a rush.

That stutter again.

Devon considered and then said, "So, I didn't really know you had a stutter. I mean, before today you've hardly said a word around me all these years, you know?"

Carl shrugged.

"Is it annoying for you?" Devon asked.

"Yes. Of course it is. Is it for you?"

"No. Of course not."

"It only happens when I have big feelings or…" Carl cleared his throat and his cheekbones glowed pink. "Or wh-when I feel out of control."

"You feel out of control right now?"

He shrugged. "I guess."

"But earlier, when I got here, you were so cool and calm."

"I was still in c-control then, because you hadn't said yes." He frowned for a moment and then said in a rush, "I could still pretend to be someone else."

"Huh?"

"It's a trick I do to keep from stuttering. My speech th-therapist t-t-taught it t-to me," Carl said. He took a slow deep breath, and that icy exterior that Devon recalled from every prior interaction with Carl dropped over him. "This. I don't stutter as much when I do this. Actors with stutters almost never have trouble with fluency on the stage, and I don't stutter when I'm on stage either—even when I'm not singing, when I'm just talking between the songs."

"Oh."

"Yeah." Carl let it go, and the coldness thawed. He cleared his throat. "My…my therapist suggested acting like I'm on ss-stage when the st-stutter is a pr-problem."

"Do you always have to act then? Like with Hope? Or your mom?"

He shook his head. "But they don't make me feel v-vulnerable like y-y—" He rolled his eyes.

"I make you feel vulnerable?"

He nodded.

Devon pondered that, and then asked, "Are there particular sounds that are harder than others?"

He took a slow breath. "Most consonants can be hard if I'm nervous. I use my breathing carefully, too. That's another str-strategy."

"When we're in bed, though, the only time you stuttered was when I was the one who—" Devon sat up straighter. "Oh. When you're in control, you don't stutter. Are you being that other person then? While we're in bed?"

He shook his head. "No. That's me."

"Then what?"

"Eat your food," he said firmly. "Suck my dick. Fuck me." He smirked. "I can say all that. It's…it's when I'm vulnerable and not in charge, or when I feel anxious. You…mm-make me feel like I might have to beg."

"Do you feel like you should beg now? Here?"

He shook his head. "I want to take charge of you. It's when I resist that, or when I don't do wh-what comes naturally, or when I feel v-v—argh." He paused and breathed in slowly. "*Vul*nerable."

Devon ate quietly for a few minutes, watching as Carl dove into his salad with gusto. He pondered his initial plans—his goals to take Carl Pink apart, to see him defenseless, and he realized he'd already done it all. He hadn't fucked him yet or been fucked by him, but he'd made him beg, he'd seen him bare, and now he had this piece of information that so few other people probably did. This slice of the real Carl Pink.

"Hey, Carl?"

He looked up.

"Be in charge." Carl's eyes shifted to a gleaming moon-color, and Devon felt breathless. "Of me. Of sex. Of this weekend. You take charge. I'll follow your lead. I already have anyway, despite my best efforts."

"You haven't li-liked…liked what we did?"

"Duh. Of course I did. Just I thought—why don't you be in charge? I'll let you."

"But would you like it?"

"Yes."

Carl nodded. "Finish your dinner. Then we'll kiss on the couch. Then you'll teach me to give better head."

Devon gulped and almost choked on a carrot from

the pot roast. "You don't want me to give you head first?"

"I want to be good at sex," Carl said firmly. "Not just have you give me good sex."

"Right, because you'll want to impress the head honchos of the music studios out there to get a record deal," Devon said a little sourly, surprised at the weird irritation he felt at the idea of Carl sucking anyone else's cock.

Carl's head tilted, and he pondered Devon for a moment before saying, "If I wanted to do that, would that bother you?"

"Fuck yeah. You shouldn't have to have sex with someone to get ahead in the world."

Carl shrugged. "I just want to give good blow jobs to whoever I end up sucking off. It's not about that. Why did you think it was?"

"I didn't," Devon said. "Not really. I just don't want to think about you sucking a lot of cocks."

Carl smiled and giggled. Devon's heart stopped and started again with a kick.

"What?"

"Nothing. I just see," Carl said.

Devon almost asked what it was Carl saw, but they both knew, so he kept his mouth shut. Silly to be getting attached after just a few shared orgasms and a confession of vulnerability. Carl had made it clear at the start he was into Devon, and it was absurd to think he could be into

Carl too, just because he liked being under his hand and bossed around in bed.

Who knew?

But the kid was leaving, and Devon had a job and a college scholarship. A few lessons in sex didn't make for strong relationship potential. Hell, it had only been *hours* so far. A few days of pleasure in the pouring rain wasn't a recipe for a happy ending. Not when Carl was on his way across the country. Not when they were still basically strangers.

But at least Devon was going to get to suck Carl's cock. At some point.

After Carl sucked his again.

Chapter Six

CARL'S MOUTH WAS big and hot, and Devon was drowning in it.

Carl wasn't a great kisser yet, by any means, and yet Devon was sure that Carl was the fastest learner in the whole world when it came to sexual practices that he'd ever met. Not that he'd had a lot of virgins (or any), but he hadn't expected to get so attached to Carl's lips so fast.

"Now," Carl said, pulling away and dropping back to his haunches where he knelt at Devon's feet.

They were both naked again, this time in the living room, sitting on a blanket spread across the sofa. The lights were turned low despite the lack of backdoor neighbors who might want to peer in. There was just forest and mountain out there, and no need for caution, but the darkness made the lushness of the way their bodies touched all the more delicious.

Devon supposed this was why most people preferred to fuck at night.

"I'm going to take hold of you," Carl said with certainty, "and put the head of your cock in my mouth. I'm going to suck it and you're going to like it."

Devon nodded, feeling tongue-tied and dizzy. He'd come so many times already in the last few hours; he shouldn't be this turned on, and his cock shouldn't be aching like it hadn't had any attention ever before. But the way Carl talked about sucking him off was arousing as fuck. Carl was matter-of-fact, like it was already a done deal, and it was so damn sexy. Devon was going to lose his mind if Carl didn't just get on with it.

"No teeth," Carl muttered to himself as he took hold of Devon's dick and leaned over it.

Devon wanted to watch, but his eyes closed as Carl's hot breath encased the head of his dick, and the sweet, slick hotness of his lips and mouth took him in. He'd told Carl to concentrate on the head for now and pump the rest of the shaft with his fist, because deep throating was a whole other thing and not really that amazing unless you were good at the basics, too.

"Get it good and sloppy wet." Devon moaned as Carl sucked and worked his tongue around the head. "Down the shaft, let the saliva—ahh, yeah, like that."

His eyes popped open, and he looked to where Carl knelt between his thighs, blond head moving in a swirling motion as the wetness of saliva slid down Devon's shaft and slicked the places Carl's fist wrapped around, working him to a higher state of arousal.

Devon's balls were already drawing up, and he suggested, "You can suck the balls. Lightly. Not too rough."

Carl pulled off his cock and huffed. "I'll get to them. Shut up. I'm drinking your pre-cum. It's hot."

Then he went back to nursing the head of Devon's cock, and Devon watched as Carl swallowed a small pulse of pre-cum brought on by the bossy order to shut up. He squirmed as Carl slid his other hand between Devon's ass cheeks and pressed a finger against his asshole.

"Slick it up first," Devon said. "If you're gonna—" He groaned. "Oh, okay, just slide it around there, that's good. Fuck."

Devon's legs started to tremble as Carl rubbed his calloused fingertips against his asshole and sucked the head of his dick like he was going to nurse his entire load straight from the tip. And, if Devon was learning anything about Carl, he would do exactly that if he wanted to and had set his mind on it.

"That's—" Devon touched Carl's hair, threading his fingers into it and massaging his scalp. "So good. Right. There. With. Your…ugh. Oh, that's—*fuck*."

He groaned as Carl popped off, leaving him on the edge of orgasm, aching and unfinished. "Why?" he whimpered. "Why do you keep doing that?"

"I like it," Carl said. He grinned. "Look at you. Sexy Devon. The guy I've jerked off thinking about for years.

Shaking for me. Waiting for *me* to let him come. I like that."

"I can get myself off," Devon said, reaching for his cock and not at all surprised when Carl grabbed his wrists and squeezed them.

"No. You'll come in my mouth. Just not yet."

Devon relaxed back, and Carl released his wrists. He pushed Devon's legs apart before he sidled between them. Carl's cock brushed Devon's stomach as he moved his way up to Devon's nipples.

"No teeth," Devon reminded, but then changed his mind as Carl took one nipple into his mouth. "Well, just a little bit of teeth."

Carl nipped and Devon squirmed.

"That's all. No more than that."

Carl flicked his tongue over the nipple and slid his hand back down to Devon's hole, rubbing the callouses over it and teasing him.

"It's too dry," Devon said. "Lick it."

Carl stuck his finger into his mouth and got it wet, then went back to teasing Devon's nipple and asshole, but this time it was even better because his finger was wet and slick. "Finger me," Devon said.

Carl huffed against his chest and bit his nipple again, but harder than before so that Devon jumped. "I'm in charge and I'll finger you when I want."

Devon's feet flexed and released. He wished he could

express how hot it was when Carl denied him, but he didn't want to admit it either, because he also wanted to come. A lot.

"Get on your knees," Carl said, moving back.

"No more practicing giving head?" Devon asked, but he did as Carl had ordered, letting Carl position him so that his knees were on the carpet, his ass was in the air, and his head rested on the blanket-draped sofa cushion, eyes squeezed shut.

"I want to rim you."

Devon stilled and said nothing. He loved being rimmed, but he wasn't going to make a big deal out of it, in case it turned out Carl didn't like it. Some guys didn't.

"Teeth?" Carl asked.

"Lightly, only very, *very* lightly."

Carl grunted and pushed Devon's ass cheeks apart and leaned in. "Mm," he murmured, running his thumb over his most tender place so that Devon shivered. "I'll be sticking my cock in there."

Devon squeezed his eyes shut and rubbed his cheek against the soft fabric of the blanket. He knew it wasn't going to happen now, but he did look forward to Carl fucking him, even if his prick was a bit bigger than Devon was accustomed to taking. It'd feel great stretching him open and—

"Ohhh," Devon moaned as Carl's lips pressed his hole with a feather-light kiss. "That's nice."

Carl chuckled and suddenly gave up any coy sweetness.

He was a rimming genius, that was all Devon could think as Carl explored all the various ways an asshole could be licked, sucked, bitten, and penetrated by a tongue. Any fear Devon had that Carl wouldn't like it disappeared as his moans competed with Devon's, and he began to add fingers to his exploration, using them to pull Devon's hole wider and push his tongue in deeper. Chills coursed over his body, and his cock grew ragingly hard, leaking onto the blanket.

"Fuck," Devon groaned when Carl reached beneath to stroke him while still working his tongue and lips all over Devon's hole. "You're fuck, Carl, you're gonna make me come."

Carl stroked faster, harder, and drove his tongue into Devon. The shivering, intense pleasure grew, and the knot of pressure in his core strengthened. He felt his asshole tighten, and then, just like that…

Carl pulled away, leaving his cock to slap against his stomach and his asshole to tremble in the cool air. Devon groaned as Carl laughed and slapped Devon's haunches. "Okay, let's take a break."

"What?" Devon nearly screeched, coming up to his elbows and looking over his shoulder at Carl in disbelief.

"Yeah. We should just chill. Talk like you wanted. Get to know each other."

Devon garbled a mess of sounds he didn't even think were words.

Carl sat on the sofa, his hard cock jutting up, and reached for the remote control on the table beside the arm of the couch. "Let's see. What's on your watchlist? I find that tells me a lot about person."

Devon's asshole tingled and ached, and his cock was about to explode. He knew he was staring at Carl like he was utterly bonkers, but that was because he was. Who did this to a person? Ate their ass, jerked them to near completion, and then started scrolling their Netflix queue? Fuck. What the fuck?

"Ah, *Schitt's Creek*. Nice. Um, but what's up with *Riverdale*? Babe, you know that went off the rails after season one, right?"

"Not my list. Hope's."

"Hope does *not* watch *Riverdale*," Carl said, shaking his head. "No way. And this is your Netflix icon with your name on it. Your list. *Lucifer*? Procedurals, even supernatural ones, are a yawn, but he's hot, so okay."

"You're really gonna just look at Netflix?" Devon croaked.

Carl shrugged. "You wanted to get to know each other. I'm trying to find out more about you."

"You said you already know me!" Devon gasped, trying to decide if he should turn sideways on the sofa and stick his ass in Carl's face. How was he supposed to react to this?

Carl patted the sofa. "Sit down. Relax. I'm gonna get you off later, but I think it would be fun if you wait."

"Fun for who?"

"For me." Carl smiled. "I like it when you're like this. Look at you. Such a mess."

Devon took the seat, his hole still dying for more touches and his dick leaking as though he hadn't had several orgasms already today. Even his nipples were screaming at the denial.

"Tell me why you're on—wow, Season Four? Wow. Season four of this horrible show, babe. Explain that."

"I think Archie's hot." Devon reached for his own cock, because, fuck, he needed to feel something on it, but Carl reached out and grabbed his hand and brought it over to *his* cock instead.

"Fair," Carl said, his head falling back a little as Devon began to pump. His voice sounded grittier than ever when he went on with, "But it's a terrible show. Admit it."

"Only if you let me come."

"Ha! Definitely not yet. Suck me."

Devon's eyes rolled up. He hadn't had Carl's dick in his mouth yet—his asshole, yes, his lips, yes, and his nipples yes, but showing off his cock-sucking skills had always been interrupted by Carl steering them off the rails into orgasm.

He scrambled onto his stomach, rubbing his cock against the blanket and positioning himself so that he could take hold of Carl's dick and tease the tip of it with his lips and tongue.

"I said suck it," Carl ordered, taking hold of Devon's hair and pulling lightly. "And stop rubbing your cock on the sofa. Now."

Devon groaned and got onto his knees, sad that the friction on his dick was gone, but the position made it easier to blow Carl's mind and cock by opening his mouth and taking him in deep.

"Fuck!" Carl shouted as he bucked up, and Devon almost gagged as Carl's dick hit the back of his throat. "Oh, my God. Is this—*fuck*—is this for fucking *real?*" He sounded both awed and almost angry, as if the pleasure of what he was feeling was enraging on some level. "Jesus Christ, Devon, ungh, holy shit."

Devon would have laughed, but his mouth was very full, and Carl had a grip on his hair that should have been irritating, but was, instead, hot as hell. His own balls ached, and his nipples tingled as he opened his mouth wide and slid farther down until his nose was buried in Carl's blond pubes. He pushed his tongue out, cradling Carl's dick and protecting it from his lower teeth.

"Ohhhh," Carl moaned. "Fuck, I was gonna tease you. Make you blow me while I watched this shitty show. But fucking hell, Devon. I don't think I can."

Devon pulled off Carl's cock and sat back on his heels. He wiped his mouth with the heel of his hand, then smiled as Carl gestured to the spot at his feet between his spread thighs. "Get down there and get back to it. Now."

"Bossy."

"Devon, do you want to come again tonight?"

"Yes."

Carl jerked his finger toward the floor again. Devon's knees were between Carl's feet in a second, and he smoothed his hands up Carl's wiry thighs and took hold of his hips to position him and went to town on his cock.

Carl writhed on the sofa, arching his back, pinching his own nipples as Devon deep-throated him again and again. He cried out with a harsh, deep vibration that rattled Devon's own cock and balls, and Carl's legs began to tremble and shake.

But he didn't come.

Devon was almost gleeful when he realized why. Carl had come too many times already; he was going to have to work for this—or Devon was—and he was going to absolutely *lose it*.

No matter how bossy he was, no matter how in control he tried to be, this was something that wasn't going to be rushed, and Devon was eager to see how unglued Carl came before he achieved another orgasm.

And he had a great idea on how to make him even more unhinged.

Saliva soaked Carl's pubic hair as Devon deep-throated him before coming up to spit on the head and let that slide down. He slicked his fingers in it and trailed them between Carl's cheeks to probe his asshole.

A push, and a shocked gasp from Carl, and he had one finger sunk into all that tight, virginal heat right up to the knuckle. More spit and a little pressure, and he was in deep enough to try to—

There.

Carl clenched Devon's hair and grunted like he'd been shot.

Devon didn't let up with sucking his cock either, angling himself so that he could bob his head and take Carl deep while shoving in to finger his prostate.

It didn't take long before Carl was sweating, shaking, and pleading with Devon—for what? Even Carl didn't seem to know. He wanted to come, but he couldn't seem to get there, and he wanted more fingers, but when he had three inside, all rubbing his prostate, he just begged even harder.

"Please, please, please," he whimpered, as he shivered and shook, his cock hard as velvet-covered iron in Devon's mouth. "Please, oh, Jesus, please. Devon…Devon…please."

The pleading was arousing, and Devon's cock flexed

on its own, leaking pre-cum onto the carpet between his knees. His balls ached, and he wanted to have a condom at hand so he could roll one on, lube up, and press into the hot, grip of Carl's body.

Instead, he worked his fingers. Rubbing Carl's prostate with abandon, until his hand hurt, and Carl was keening and convulsing, his asshole seizing and his legs quaking as his knees drew up.

Rolling his tongue over the leaking head of Carl's sensitive cock, Devon tasted the ongoing release of pre-cum, the tangy flavor of Carl's seed, and he wanted to feel it pulse against his tongue, shoot into his throat and slip over his lips as his mouth filled with it.

Carl whined, hunching, and his eyes opened. He twisted his fingers into Devon's hair, holding him still and steady. He stared into his eyes with that crystal-blue gaze, and gritted out, "Don't move. Hold still."

Devon stopped his fingers, froze his mouth in place, and gazed at Carl for a long moment.

"Now," Carl said, urgently. "Again."

Devon moved his fingers and sucked hard, not at all shocked when Carl gripped his head and thrust up, shooting into his throat. He gobbled what he could, trying to keep any being wasted, but of course, just as he'd imagined, his mouth overflowed and cum dripped down Carl's cock, coating his balls and slipping to aid Devon's fingers as they fucked in and out of Carl's gripping hole.

"Fuck," Carl groaned as he collapsed back, trembling. "Holy fuck."

Devon was about to die now, his cock screaming for release. He climbed onto the sofa, straddling Carl's hips, and got to his feet. Standing over Carl, he was dizzy with need, but he was able to bend his knees, grip the back of the sofa with one hand, and press his cock against Carl's lips. "Please," he whimpered, and Carl opened for him. Jerking himself hard and fast, Devon's body clenched as he unloaded almost hurtful spurts of jizz into Carl's eagerly sucking mouth.

Groaning, Devon sank down, nipples singing, cock thudding, and balls roaring. He felt Carl's cock pressing against his stomach as they panted together. They'd toppled over, gripping each other like a lifeline and breathing like they might start crying.

"Wow," Carl said. "I think I came so hard my eyeballs shot out my dick."

"Me too."

"Is it always this good?" Carl asked. "When I get to LA, will the guys I fuck make me come like this?"

Devon trembled in Carl's arms as he considered it. Had *he* ever come like this with anyone before? Never. Most of his sexual experiences had been pleasurable, fun, but this was as if he were peeling back layers of himself he hadn't known existed and uncovering his real self underneath. This was like being scrubbed raw and rediscovering the meaning of life. This was epiphany after epiphany.

And he was having it with a virgin.

Well, former virgin.

No way was Carl a virgin now.

"Devon?" Carl asked uncertainly. "Will they? Make me feel this good?"

Devon cleared his throat. "Maybe. I don't know. They could, I guess." God, he hoped not. He didn't want Carl begging anyone but him for anything at all. He didn't want Carl arching on anyone else's fingers. Or swallowing anyone else's cum.

"I don't think they will," Carl said, and he sounded a little devastated. "I think this is the best it gets."

Devon was silent. He didn't know what to say. It was the best he'd ever gotten, and he wasn't able to deny that. But he also didn't know what to do with the sadness in Carl's voice.

The kid was leaving. Devon had school.

It was this weekend and nothing more.

There was no time to waste. No orgasm to leave unexperienced. This could be the best sex either of them ever had. This and only this.

"C'mon," Devon said. "Let's go upstairs. If we start up again, I'm going to fuck you. For that, we'll need supplies."

Carl gripped Devon closer. "In a minute. Rest now. We have all weekend."

Devon settled in, but the anxiety didn't leave his heart. They *did* have all weekend. But what was he supposed to do about the fact that he knew deep down that wasn't going to be long enough.

"IT'S F-FINE. NO, it's good. No, I mean it. It's g-good. For real. Yes."

Devon woke to the sound of Carl's whispers and opened his eyes to see him standing naked by the back window, staring out at the night forest, his cell phone pressed to his ear.

"Hope, he's great. J-just like I knew he would be. I'm fine. You worry too m-much."

He sighed.

"I'm st-stuttering because I think I'm going to regret this for the r-rest of my l-life." He wiped a hand over his face. "B-because it's *too* good. I think our chemistry is…it's…we're…ugh, I can't say it. No, n-not because of the s-stutter. Because it's too real."

Carl straightened his shoulders. "No! I want this!" He huffed. "You're missing the point. He's amazing. The point is I could love him. I might already love him. No, it's not just orgasms t-talking. It's m-me."

Devon closed his eyes quickly when Carl shifted so he was looking toward the sofa, watching Devon "sleep."

"I don't know. He's everything I knew he was, and then he's somehow more." Carl scoffed. "I can't tell you! Because he's your brother. B-because it's p-private, even if he wasn't."

He sighed. "He looks so sweet when he's asleep. Did you know? Ugh. Well, you're his sister. You would think so. Shut up. No. I won't tell you more and you don't want to know more." His stutter had cleared up. He sounded more like his usual self—arrogant, cold. "Thanks for calling, Hope, but I'm fine. This is good. I'm glad I did it. And I'm sad as fuck."

He must have disconnected the call then, because he sat at the side of the sofa, his hip touching Devon's and he stroked Devon's arm, down to his fingers before taking hold of Devon's hand.

"Wake up, sleeping beauty," he said softly. "Let's go up to your room now. The bed will be more comfortable."

"For fucking or sleeping?" Devon asked as he pretended to wake up.

"Either."

Devon didn't argue.

The house was dark as he followed Carl up the stairs, letting him lead the way to Devon's room as if the place was his and not the other way around.

In the darkness, the bed was a sweet, soft oasis, and they settled onto it together. Carl pressed up to Devon's side, his soft cock against Devon's thigh.

As it turned out, the move to the bed was for sleeping, and Devon discovered that he liked sleeping with someone else next to him. It was soothing and intimate.

For something that was only going to last the weekend, this with Carl was strangely real. He loved it. And he hated it.

And he wanted more.

FRIDAY

Chapter Seven

D AWN WOKE THEM along with their morning wood, which they satisfied by clinging to each other and rubbing off while kissing.

Then they went downstairs, wearing actual clothes for the first time since Carl had stripped his shirt off—though they were just sweatpants and T-shirts—to consider breakfast.

"Do you think I need to use the douche I packed?" Carl asked as he watched Devon open a box of Pop Tarts. "So that everything's…you know…c-clean d-down there?"

"Shit happens," Devon said matter-of-factly as he put two Pop Tarts into the toaster and pushed the lever down.

He broke out the almond milk next and poured them both glasses. He supposed the lack of cow milk was also due to something either Carl or Hope had read online about anal cleanliness. He didn't know for sure, but it worked for him, since dairy had started to upset his stomach in the last few months.

"Especially if you're a gay guy. It just does sometimes. It's okay. Don't get embarrassed about it. But honestly, your butt's gonna be pretty clean if you're not feeling an actual urge to shit. That's all stored up higher, you know."

Carl frowned. "But I don't want it to gross you out."

"It won't." Devon said. "I'll be way too busy thinking about hot it is to fuck your ass to worry about a little shit. If it even happens."

Carl smirked. "How's my ass compare to that ex of yours?"

To be honest, Carl's butt was a little flat, but Devon was so eager to get inside it, that it was still the hottest ass he'd ever seen. "No comparison. Yours beats it."

"Really?" Carl seemed doubtful, but he hadn't stuttered, so Devon took that as a sign he was feeling relaxed despite the topic of conversation.

Devon didn't know if he should confess this or not, but having heard Carl's open conversation with Hope the night before, he felt that sharing his own vulnerability was only fair. He cleared his throat. "You make me come like I'm having an out of body experience. Don't know why. I mean, you're new at all this. So it can't be your skills—"

Carl choked on a laugh. "I'm that bad?"

"No! I just mean—it's not like you're doing anything advanced."

"Yeah," Carl nodded. "I know."

"You know?"

"I guess it's ch-chemistry. You and me. Like together we make it more. Just…m-m-more."

"Yeah," Devon agreed, turning to pull the hot Pop Tarts from the toaster and putting them on plates, passing one to Carl. "Chemistry. Compatibility. It's something. I just—fuck, I'm getting hard now," he said, laughing. "I've never come so many times in a row and still gotten hard. Hell, I've never come so many times with anyone ever."

Carl reached down and obviously adjusted his own dick before putting his elbows on the counter. "But it's not love," he said firmly. "Because we can't love each other yet, right? Because we don't know each other well enough."

"I thought you knew everything about me," Devon teased.

"I had to reassess that when I saw *Riverdale* on your fucking watchlist."

Devon laughed. "C'mon, surely you watch something questionable too."

Carl shrugged. "*Cobra Kai.*"

Devon nudged him. "Who do you think is hot on it?"

"No one. I just like the show."

"It was fun for the first two seasons."

"Third season, though?" Carl shook his head. "Jumped the shark."

"Mm?" Devon's mouth was full of Pop Tart.

"Means it lost the thread of the story, basically, or it became so bad it's not even good. Or whatever. I don't know. My mom says it." Carl waved his hand. "But back to us and sex. We could have it again sometime, couldn't we? When I come back to visit my parents or whatever?"

Devon was tempted to agree to the proposal, but he also knew that if this really wasn't a thing that could last, he should just enjoy what he could this weekend, feel all this super-hot pleasure, and then let it go. See if he could find something like it with someone he could build a relationship with. Not someone who was going three thousand miles away to chase a dream that didn't include being with him.

"Maybe," Devon said, because his mouth wouldn't say no.

I mean, the way he makes you come, his brain whispered.

"Yeah, we'll see," Carl said, but it was clear he was disappointed. He broke his remaining Pop Tart into four pieces and popped one into his mouth, chewing.

They were silent as they finished eating, and Devon felt like an idiot, but he had to bring it up. "I'm still hard."

Carl smiled. "Me too."

They stared at each other over the counter before Carl rose, his sweats bulging in the front. "I came here to get my ass fucked. You still haven't done that. Upstairs. Now. Condom on. Let's do it."

Devon swallowed hard, the click audible in the otherwise quiet kitchen, and they ditched the plates and left their crumbs on the counter.

Being on the north side of the house, Devon's bedroom was still dark, especially with the blinds down. Carl entered the room behind him, already taking off his shirt.

Devon fetched the condoms and lube and put them on his bedside table next to his old football clock he'd gotten from Santa one Christmas. When he turned around, Carl was naked, and hard, and staring at him with a commanding expression.

"Get the condom on," Carl said. "I don't want to toy around today. I want to get fucked."

"I should prep you first," Devon said, his voice shaking, which was super weird since he was not the ass virgin here. He shrugged out of his shirt and kicked off his sweatpants.

"Then get to it." Carl dropped onto the bed, lay on his back, and lifted his legs behind the knees, spreading himself wide.

After tearing open a condom with shaking hands and rolling it onto his dick, Devon fell onto the bed, too, his mouth open and ready, eager to get his lips and tongue on Carl's hole again. The condom felt annoying since he wasn't in Carl yet, but he ignored it as he licked and sucked, and began to finger Carl's asshole.

Just like the day before, Carl's legs began to shake, his feet flexed, and he growled and cried out with pleasure while Devon worked him open. Each stroke over his prostate had him cursing with that same near-anger he'd had when Devon had given him head and fingered him the night before.

"Hurry," Carl said, his deep, dark voice rolling over Devon with an urgency. "Fuck this prep stuff. Get your cock inside me."

Devon wasn't sure Carl was ready, but he didn't have a way to stop himself now. He was already on his knees, his condom-wrapped dick aiming for Carl's slicked-up hole, and he leaned in—

Carl's eyes went wide and then rolled up, his ass opening around the head of Devon's cock. His asshole flared as Devon pressed inside. "Fuuuuuck," he groaned, twisting and bearing down to take it deeper. "Fuuuuuuuck."

Carl's ass gripped and released, pulling him in as Devon pressed forward. Goosebumps raised over Devon's body as he seated himself in Carl.

"Okay?" Devon gritted out. His hips were flexed and tense. He wanted to drag out slowly and throw himself forward into Carl again, but he held very, very still. "You okay?"

Carl groaned and his ass tensed around Devon. His knuckles were white on the backs of his knees, and his feet were flexed. Then he let out a slow, trembling breath. His hole lost some grip, and his body relaxed some. "Do it," he commanded. "Move."

Devon shifted back, sliding out until just the head of his cock was still in Carl's gripping body, and then he pushed back in. Again. Again.

Carl tossed his head. His entire chest and neck were pink, and his nipples were so rosy that Devon could barely hold back from bending over to taste them. But he resisted. He wanted Carl to feel this fuck. To not lose himself in other sensations. To remember the first time he had a cock in his ass, and to always know it was Devon's.

"Move faster," Carl said, breathless and shaking. His eyes gleamed like eclipsed blue-white moons around his blown pupils. "Harder."

Devon obeyed, leaning to rest his hands on either side of Carl's writhing body as he shoved in again and again, rubbing Carl's prostate, as evidenced by his throaty shouts and shattered expression each time he nailed it.

Devon wasn't anywhere close to coming himself. The overload of orgasms the day before seemed to be holding over to the morning, and he stroked in and out of Carl harder, faster, and with a rhythm that typically would have made him shoot his load in minutes. Not today.

Carl seemed on the verge of leaving his body. He struggled and gasped, he whined and shouted, and his asshole convulsed around Devon's cock with a wild, pulsing grip.

He kicked Devon once, like he was a horse Carl demanded gallop faster, and he spasmed against the bed when Devon obeyed his urging with a particularly intense thrust. The way he shook and trembled, it was as if he was being fucked apart, every ounce of his usual reserve vanished as he caught Devon's cock over and over. Carl seemed broken open with heat, lust, and demand, his expression shattering with desire and beautiful need.

Devon soaked all that in, driving into Carl, fucking him harder than he probably should have fucked a virgin, and yet Carl kicked him again when he slowed down, making him gallop, making him ride him into the mattress.

Carl sought his own cock and Devon smiled. He wasn't going to jerk Carl off this time. Another fuck, maybe, but this time he was going to make Carl get himself off while Devon did the work of making Carl's asshole sing praises to Jesus and all the saints. Which he seemed to be doing a good job of, because Carl was wailing now. Absolutely wailing as he stroked himself and sought release.

A wicked thought came to him, and Devon watched as Carl brought himself closer, closer, and—

Devon grabbed his hand away, keeping him from going over the edge.

Carl snarled. "You—oh, fuck you."

Devon laughed. "I want you to remember this fuck and who made you come for the rest of your life."

Carl's eyes glowed. "Like I'd forget." His hips twitched and he shook all over, his eyes rolling up, his thighs going berserk with trembling. "What the fuck is that? Why does that happen?" he said. "It keeps. Oh fuck. Happening."

And it did. Again.

Devon grinned, his hips snapping, his cock hot and bright with pleasure, and his own balls drawing up. He'd never experienced what it was clear Carl was going through. But he knew some men who had. And on his first fuck. Jesus their chemistry was unreal. This was unheard of. The two of them should not be this hot together. Hell.

"Just ride it," he suggested.

Carl shot him a look that told him to fuck off, but then he groaned again, and his legs kicked as he convulsed once more. "Jesus," he screamed. "Fuck."

"Stroke yourself," Devon said.

Carl glared up at him. "I'm in control," he gritted out. "I'm the one who—" His eyes rolled back again, and Devon almost laughed. Carl grabbed his own cock and in a few rough strokes he was shouting, his head back, and his body gripping enough Devon had to stop thrusting and instead shove deep and let Carl come apart on his cock.

Jizz flew up all over Carl's chest and into his hair.

It even hit Devon under the chin.

Tears stood in Carl's eyes when he shuddered his way back down again, and gazed up at Devon. His cheeks were as pink as roses and his nipples were red like cayenne. Devon bent to lick them. Carl jolted under him.

"Fuck you," Carl said quietly.

"Mm?" Devon asked, pulling away, worried and gazing into Carl's bright eyes.

"I know that's not normal. I know that was *too* good. Come to L.A. with me. Fuck me forever."

Devon huffed a laugh. Orgasms were known for bringing on love declarations, but this? Instead of answering he dislodged himself, removed the condom, and started jerking himself off, aiming for Carl's already jizz-covered chest.

It took longer than he wanted it to, but he was still yelling to God above when he shot onto Carl's pink skin. He collapsed beside him, and they kissed. It was slow and sexy, and Devon found himself wondering just how much was tuition at UCLA anyway?

Just how much was he willing to risk for more of this with Carl? For sex that made him want to take the other person to heights never seen? For orgasms that felt like brand new bliss?

Could there really be more to life than this?

Right now, high and wrung out, he didn't think so.

Chapter Eight

"WHAT'S YOUR DREAM in life?" Carl asked from where he sat on the cushion-covered swing on the back patio, playing his guitar.

They'd taken a break from all the madness after they'd fucked, and now they were outside touching grass, so to speak. Devon literally so. He stood barefoot in the yard, head tilted back, watching clouds drift overhead and admiring how the treetops scraped the blue as they waved in the light wind.

The rain had stopped the night before, and the grass had dried in the sun while they'd been in Devon's bedroom getting sticky together. Now it stroked the soles of his feet as Devon considered Carl's question.

"I don't know. I guess I keep hoping college will make all that clear to me. Right now, I just know I don't want to do anything that requires any more math classes."

Carl smiled, picking away at his guitar, making a pretty melody. "Have you declared a major?"

Devon winced. "Yeah. English literature. I don't

know why? Like, I have no career aspirations in that area. I just like reading and thinking about what I've read. I look forward to my classes. But I don't know. It's not like I want to become a teacher, or a writer, or anything like that."

"Yeah." Carl kept playing, and when Devon turned to him, he felt a weird clench in his chest.

Carl was a beautiful guy. The blondest parts of his hair shone in the sunlight, and his skin just glowed. He was so damn gorgeous, even if his eyes were tired when he looked up. There was no ice prince in his expression now.

Devon could chalk it up to the sex, to tearing down Carl's barriers with the power of cock and orgasm, but he felt like it was more than that. It was more like Carl himself was a soft man, and that brittle exterior was just an act. Which would explain a lot about his friendship with Hope. His sister didn't have terrible taste in friends after all.

"What about you?" Devon asked. "I mean, it's music obviously, but what's your *dream*-dream?"

Carl shrugged. "Believe it or not, I don't really have one. I don't necessarily want to make it big or be a star. I just want to play good music and be part of something bigger than me." No stutter. Not even a little bit. He was secure in this and relaxed, and Devon felt proud that Carl was showing all of himself this way. "I want to keep my options open, you know? Like I could see myself as a studio musician, but I don't have to go to L.A. for that. I could try for that dream in Nashville."

"Why not Nashville then?"

Carl picked the melody a bit more, his eyes going distant. "I'm an only child, you know that, and I love my parents. But part of me just wants to see what happens if I'm far away from them. Can I make it on my own? I guess I want a big adventure. Nashville just doesn't seem like a big enough change. Los Angeles, though. That's a whole new world in some ways. And what if it doesn't stop there?" His expression grew a bit more avid. "What if I find an opportunity that takes me even further away? To, I don't know, Seoul, or Sydney, or London?"

"There're opportunities like that in the music world?"

"Sure. Touring musicians, for example. Or if I got into more serious songwriting, there are opportunities that way, too. I'm young, you know? I don't have to set a course forever right now. I just know the general direction I want to go in and I'm going to trust I can find my way."

Devon stepped onto the patio, sitting on the swing next to Carl. They rocked back and forth in silence as the music trailed from Carl's guitar. "You have a lot of faith in the future," Devon said.

"You don't?"

"I don't know. I just always felt like I needed to follow the right path. Whatever *right* is, you know? Be a good older brother, be a good son and student, go to college, get a job to help pay for school. I just figured eventually I'd see some clear future for myself, but I really don't. I thought I was weird for that—everyone else always seems to know what they want to do: become a doctor, a dancer, an actress. Like, even if their dreams are unlikely to come true, at least they have a dream. Hope, for instance, and her plan to get her engineering degree and work for the Tennessee Valley Authority. Like she has this clear vision."

"She's going to have the most boring life," Carl said on a sigh. "I keep telling her to dream bigger, but she's dead set on it. Which I guess I also admire. I just hope she doesn't end up a frog in a well, you know? Trapped in a small world."

"Hope likes small things," Devon said. "She'll be fine."

Carl shrugged.

"But what I hear you saying is you don't have a clear vision either. You're winging it just like the rest of us. Just winging it in a different direction and down another path."

Carl chuckled and put his guitar aside, laying it carefully on the patio before turning to Devon. "What if you came with me? To Los Angeles?"

"Ha! Right!"

"I'm serious. Why not?"

"Because, well, we're just fucking for the weekend?"

Their first conversation in the entryway came flooding back to Devon's mind, and Carl's worry that if they got to know each other he would have hope for more. Despite the weekend thus far playing out much more like Carl's original vision, maybe Devon had let hope grow in Carl too, by accident.

Hopeless hope.

"Right, that's true, but what if we fuck for longer than that?" Carl asked, reaching out and taking Devon's hand. "What if you took next semester off and came out to L.A. and had a big adventure with me. You know I'm good for some amazing sex, and who knows what else you might find out there with me? What if you find something you love? Something that you can envision yourself doing long-term?"

"What? Like acting?"

Carl touched Devon's stubbly chin and grinned. "Well, you're gorgeous enough for that, but if the acting bug hasn't bitten you yet, I doubt it's going to. No, but maybe something else. There are all kinds of careers in the world, but most of the time we don't know about them. Like did you know I could get a gig on a cruise ship as a musician? Go all over the world. And you could get a job as a waiter, since you have experience, and we could see so many places all while earning a living. That's just one example. There are so many options, Devon. It doesn't have to be O'Charley's and college, and sex with guys that isn't half as good as sex with me."

"So cocky for a virgin," Devon said, his heart pounding and his hands shaking a little, because Carl was making him think. Like *really* think. For the first time ever. About what life might exist outside of their part of the country, and all that Devon had ever known of the world.

"Just imagine—the weather in Los Angeles in January is much better than here. We could drive across the country together—we'll take the southern route because, you know, so much snow otherwise—and we'd see sites, fuck in hotel rooms, explore. We'd get to know each other, too. Real fast. That'd be fun, wouldn't it? And hot? I've always thought fucking in some dumb roadside motel room has a kind of gross appeal, you know? Like grungy hot."

"You're serious?"

"Of course."

"How long have you been thinking about this?"

Carl smiled. "Just a few hours, but it's a great idea, isn't it? Just because it's a new one, doesn't mean it's a bad one."

No stuttering. Steady, flowing, easy speech. No ice prince in sight. No fake persona to keep the stuttering at bay, either. Carl was comfortable with Devon in a way he never had been before, obviously, and equally obvious was the understanding that Carl meant every word.

"Like, really? Drop out of school?"

"Maybe not for good. I mean, we might hate each other in the end. Moving across country. Living in a new city. I say just take a semester off, a sabbatical, and come out there with me. See how it goes. You can always come back and pick up where you left off if it doesn't work out. But if it does work out—there are community colleges and schools out there. Other job opportunities. Like I said, the options are limitless and open."

"But how will we afford to live there?" Devon asked, having bought into the fantasy long enough to spot the biggest, most obvious problem.

"Only child, sole benefactor of a trust left to me by my grandfather, plus I do plan to work you know. So could you. It'll be a small apartment, but it'll be doable."

"You are wild," Devon said.

"How so?"

"This is—you're so—" Devon gestured at Carl, indicating the entirety of him. "You're serious?"

"Deadly."

"I don't know. I need to think about it."

"Okay," Carl said, picking up the guitar again. "Think about it. But don't think too long. If you're coming out there with me, I'll save my new-found sex skills just for you. But if you're not, then I'll probably start looking as soon as I get to L.A., you know. I mean, wouldn't want to get rusty at what I've just learned. Practice makes perfect and all that."

"That's not how sex works."

Carl smirked and shrugged. "Nevertheless, I'm going to see if other guys make me come like you do. Maybe I'm just really good at having orgasms and it's got nothing to do with your dick or our chemistry at all. Maybe any guy can make me scream like that."

Devon gritted his teeth. Carl was teasing him, obviously, but also there was no way Devon wanted to even think about Carl writhing around on some other guy's cock. Not now, not next week, not next month.

Which was absurd. This was a deflowerment. He was punching Carl's v-card six ways to Sunday and that was it.

But now he was considering dropping out of college and going cross-country to live with this tight, hot, sexy twink of a dreamer, and even though he'd said he needed to think about it, some part of his mind was already there. Already in Los Angeles on a big adventure, making a new life, finding new opportunities, and banging the ever-loving shit out of Carl Pink every chance he got.

"Fuck," Devon muttered, as Carl stood with his guitar and reached for Devon's hand.

"Exactly," Carl said quietly. "Let's go fuck."

Devon swallowed hard, gazing up at Carl, who laughed at his expression.

"What? Not up for more yet?"

"What's the plan?"

"Me in you, or you in me. I'm good either way."

Devon wasn't sure what he wanted more, to get back inside Carl and see him come unglued again, or to have Carl inside him, and get to see the kid enjoy the heat of an ass gripping his cock for the first time.

"You in me," Devon muttered.

Carl's eyes lit up. "Lead the way."

They headed into the house, stashing Carl's guitar in the living room, and started up the stairs.

Devon was so excited, his legs by the time they got to his bedroom.

Day two, Round two was about to commence.

Chapter Nine

DEVON DIDN'T KNOW what he'd expected, but lying on his back with his legs pulled up, staring at Carl's face as he pushed his cockhead experimentally against the slicked rim of Devon's asshole was turning out to be a singularly erotic experience.

The way emotions flitted over Carl's features: anxiety, trepidation, excitement, lust, hunger, and, oh God, that moment when his crown began to breach Devon's body, the all-encompassing awe that swept over his face? It was delicious.

And the trembling, the way he bit into his lower lip and squeezed his eyes shut, fighting the urge to shove in, or maybe to come, Devon wasn't sure, all lit a wild flame inside him that he'd never felt while being fucked before.

Burning lust, yes, tenderness, of course, but urgent, proprietary rage? No. Never before.

All he knew was that he wanted this from Carl now, and next week, and next month. He wanted Carl shaking as his cock sunk deeper into Devon for the rest of his life. Because nothing had ever been as right as this moment.

This rare, raw moment of joining.

Raw emotionally, not skin on skin, because Devon had fucked around with a pal all too recently to be sure of his STD status, but that was another thing Devon realized he wanted: bareback sex. Condoms in the trash. Just them and skin and lube and cum, and all of it messy between them.

"This…this okay?"

Devon didn't know if that was a stutter or just a simple verbal slip due to being overwhelmed. Because there was no doubt Carl was drowning in the sensation of his dick inside Devon's body. He was practically drooling, and his eyes were half-drooping shut as he struggled to hold steady and ask after Devon's comfort.

"Go for it," Devon said, hitching his legs back farther. "I can take it."

Taking it was easier said than done, because Carl was hung. His cock was like so many twinks': thick from the base all the way to the crown, almost like a fucking eggplant, and stretching around that girth was testing Devon's limits right now. But he wanted Carl to fuck him with abandon, to lose control, and it wasn't as if he was the virgin here. He could take it. He just needed to re—

"Oh, fuck." Devon groaned, his neck arching and his nipples aching as a zing of pleasure arced through him. "Jesus Christ."

Carl's hips stuttered but he kept thrusting as he asked, "G-good fuck? B-bad fuck?"

"Holy fuck," Devon said as Carl's dick rolled right over his prostate, milking a pulse of pre-cum from Devon's slit.

"Good then," Carl said.

That seemed to be all it took for him to find his control and certainty. He began to fuck into Devon like he was an expert instead of an innocent, and he was grinning smugly every time Devon was able to pull his eyes out from the eternal roll to the back of his head to gaze up at Carl's face.

"Look at you," Carl murmured. "Writhing on my dick." He batted Devon's hands away when he reached to touch his own dick. "Ah-ah-ah, none of that. I plan to fuck you like you fucked me. Make you come on my dick alone."

"Oh God!" Devon's body convulsed, and his eyes rolled up again. "I don't do—oh, Jesus—do that."

"Hmm," Carl sounded unconvinced. "Do you always spurt pre-cum like this when you're getting fucked?" He asked, slipping a finger through the pool on Devon's stomach before bringing it up to lick. "Mm. So good. Maybe I'll suck you off when it's over, then, if you don't come this way."

"I—don't—know," Devon grunted out between thrusts, his nerve endings lighting up again and again with every snap of Carl's greedy hips. He wasn't sure what he was feeling actually, because Carl was right. No one else's cock had ever quite worked his prostate like this during anal. He'd never felt like he was about to ascend out of his body and burst into a glitter storm that rained on the man fucking him. But that was how he felt now.

"Look at you," Carl murmured again. "Never thought I'd get to see this. It's better than I imagined. You're so hot. Slick. Tight." He gritted his teeth and clenched his hands on Devon's thighs. "Don't make me come," he said, almost angrily. "Don't want to come yet."

"Fuck," Devon whimpered, his balls buzzing and aching, his cockhead sliding over the fur of his treasure trail with each of Carl's hard thrusts. He was so turned on, so sensitive and aroused, that he wondered if he might come just from that friction alone. That and the shattering pleasure of Carl's cock rubbing his prostate.

"That's right, that's right," Carl encouraged as Devon began to shake, his limbs losing coordination. "Show me. Show me all you've got."

Devon whimpered as he twisted on Carl's cock, trying to come to grips with the sensation that was swallowing him, the buzz swelling inside his body and pressing against his skin, jittering through his muscles so that he convulsed wildly, before splintering—

Hot, wild, screamingly good.

Devon came down to earth again groaning, clutching Carl to his chest, and still taking his cock. His legs shook, his asshole continued to spasm, and he felt sure he'd shot his load, but he couldn't quite focus enough to check. He hung onto Carl and breathed in his scent, kissed his neck and moaned as the sensation began to grow again. How was he not too sensitive to continue? He should be begging Carl to pull out now, not hoping for more.

"You are so hot," Carl growled in his ear. "So fucking gorgeous." He reached between them to stroke Devon's hot, aching cock, and Devon realized he hadn't nutted yet after all. Carl moved his hand away again, though he kept close, so that with every thrust into Devon he scraped his hard stomach over Devon's needy cock.

"Let's come now," Carl said, smoothing his hands over Devon's cheeks and touching his lips with his own. "And when you move to L.A. with me, we'll do this all the time, without condoms, and I'll put my load in you, and you'll carry me around inside."

"Fucking hell," Devon groaned and pushed his hips up to catch Carl's cock.

"You want that? To carry my jizz inside of you? Part of me."

"You're filthy," Devon muttered. "Just make me come."

"Mm-hmm. I will, baby. Don't worry. I'll make you come, and when I do, you'll thank me."

"Thank you?" Devon said. "Why?"

"You'll see."

Carl thrust into him hard twice more, burying his face in Devon's neck, and crying out, "Oh, fuck! Fuck!"

Devon felt the thud of Carl's cock against his stretched hole and wished like hell all of Carl's filthy talk could have been true. He'd love to keep Carl's cum inside. To hold it in his body even after Carl was gone.

But no.

The full condom looked miserable on the end of Carl's dick, and he worked it off, aimed for the wastebasket by the bed, missed, and didn't bother trying to clean it up. Instead, he turned to Devon, a devilish expression on his otherwise spent face.

"Get ready to beg," Carl said.

"Why?" Devon said. "I mean please? Please let me come now." He didn't want to be tortured into coming, and yet when Carl sank between his legs, shoving them back and up, and went to town on his still stretched hole, he lost all ability to speak or protest. This was all he wanted, all he needed, and he didn't need to come. That was for losers.

But after a few minutes, he reversed course. His cock was so hard it was killing him, and his balls were aching too. "Please," he whispered. "Help me come."

"Yeah? Okay, well, will this get you off?" Carl asked, moving up to lick around the base of Devon's dick, and suck on his balls lightly. "That good enough?"

"No! For fuck's sake, Carl." He took hold of his own cock, but Carl pulled his fingers off one by one.

"All right, don't panic," Carl said, soothingly. "I'll help you come. All right? Let me help."

Devon's breath came in harsh stutters, and he realized that tears were pooling in his eyes. His cock and balls hurt, and he was starting to feel like he was strung out on some kind of drug, because he was still shaking from the drubbing Carl had given his prostate.

"There, there," Carl said, breathing against the head of Devon's cock. "Let me help, baby. I'm here for you." He licked the crown and gobbled up the pre-cum. "So good. You're so good. Let's get you ready to come, all right?" he said, and smeared some of Devon's cum, pooled on his stomach again, over two of his fingers. Devon's legs twitched as Carl pushed those fingers into his ass and began to rub his prostate again.

"Christ," Devon said, pressing the heels of his palms into his eyes and writhing as the electric pleasure buzzed through him and grew into a heady rushing desperation.

"Mm," Carl said, licking the head of Devon's cock and sucking at the slit. "Tastes so good."

Devon almost shouted with despair and arousal when he realized Carl was milking him and eating the cum as it leaked out. He didn't want to be milked, he wanted to shoot his load. But Carl worked his prostate with a deliberate rhythm that made Devon pulse with need and release streams of pre-cum, but he didn't suck him hard or deep enough to let him get off.

"Please," he whispered. "I want to stop if you don't let me come. I meant it. Please, Carl. Please."

Carl looked up, concern in his eyes, and he said, "Of c-course. I'm s-sorry. I was pl-playing."

"Just. Make. Me. Come." Devon gritted out. "Make. Me."

"Yeah, okay," Carl said, working Devon's prostate even harder and taking hold of the base of his cock with his other hand. He opened his mouth and started sucking the head, sweet and perfect, twirling his tongue the way Devon had told him he liked, and...

"Yes!" Devon cried, arching so hard that his back cracked, and came with powerful, hard spurts that made tears rise in his eyes. "Fuck! Thank you! Fuck!"

Carl sucked him dry before easing him down, pulling his fingers free only when Devon's twitches shifted from pleasurable aftershocks to discomfort.

"Sorry," Carl said, snuggling up to Devon on the bed.

Devon's asshole felt like the center of the universe, and his brain like a no-man's land. The usual scenario reversed.

It vaguely occurred to Devon that Carl was apologizing for something. For the weekend? For fucking him? For what? He didn't know now. He was buzzing with afterglow, his entire soul blissed out, and his nerve-endings singing hallelujah.

"Mm?" he managed.

"Sorry I made you want to stop."

"Stop?" Devon asked. He had no memory of wanting to stop, or of anything aside from sheer ecstasy leading up to an obliterating orgasm, and some sweet, tender memories of Carl's expression as he'd pushed into Devon for the first time. Pleasure had wiped the rest clean. "Never stop."

Carl huffed. "You said you'd want to stop if I didn't let you come."

Devon nodded. He *had* said that hadn't he? And coming had been so good, so he was glad he'd demanded it. "Yeah," he murmured, "But you don't need to apologize for it. I'm fine. We're fine."

"Just now, you said 'never stop,'" Carl said, nuzzling at Devon's hair and kissing his temple. "Do you mean it? You want to fuck me beyond this weekend?"

Devon shuddered. He couldn't imagine not fucking Carl again. "Yes."

"So you'll come to L.A.?"

"I don't know?" Devon wasn't going to commit to that while he was shaking from sex. No way. "Later.

We'll talk later."

Carl cuddled close and Devon felt his gaze as he drifted off but couldn't keep himself from falling asleep. He knew Carl was watching, and he hoped he didn't drool, but if he was going to move in with him in L.A., then Carl was gonna see a lot about Devon.

A little drool was no big deal in the scheme of things.

Chapter Ten

"YEAH, HE'S GREAT," Carl said, his voice low as Devon drifted back into consciousness.

Carl stood outside the bedroom door, probably so as not to disturb Devon with his phone call, though he'd left it cracked open, so Devon could hear every word.

"I don't know if he'll really come with me, but I hope he does," Carl said to whoever he was talking with. Devon assumed it was Hope.

He sat up, putting on a pair of sweatpants and standing just behind the door, listening some more.

"What is love, really?" Carl scoffed. "I mean, sure I've been half in love with him for years, but I'm not idiot enough to believe that he's in love with me just because the sex has been amazing. Yes, amazing. Like wow, Hope, did you know how good sex was? You've been holding out on me."

He huffed a laugh. "Well, that guy was a prick, and I can't believe you let him fuck you. So of course it sucked. What about Rowan, though? Surely, he was able to make you come? No? Oh, babe, you need to find someone who can make you come like Devon makes me come."

He grew quiet as Hope talked. "Well, what about Gabby Schaeffer? Rumor amongst the LGBT group at school was that she could make girls come apart with her tongue." He huffed. "Well, stop being so straight! It's ruining your sex life!"

Devon did not want to hear more about his sister's sex life. He'd only been eavesdropping to hear what Carl was saying about him, and this was way more information than he needed or wanted.

He started to open the door and—

"I think I'm a switch, because it was good both ways."

Fine, Devon would listen a little longer then.

"But when he's inside me, I think there's nothing better. *But* when I was inside him, I thought the same thing, you know? Nothing better than this. *Nothing.* Ugh, fine, fine, no more sex talk. What are you guys up to this weekend? Ah, board games. Exciting." He laughed. "No, no, I'm sorry. You can't get deflowered by the sexy guy you've crushed on for years *every* weekend, I guess. It's true. I'm sure there are plenty of board games in my future. In L.A. with your hot brother. Loser gets to top."

"Stop talking to my sister," Devon said, swinging the door open.

Carl jumped and squeaked, a noise Devon had never

imagined him making.

Devon laughed and took the phone out of his hands as Carl stared on in surprise. "He's fine. I'm taking good care of him. Don't call again."

"He called me!" Hope exclaimed.

"Well, don't answer again. I have things to do to him. Things you don't want to know about."

Hope gagged. "You're gross."

"You planned this with him."

"I know but…ugh. Bye. Have fun." She gagged again. "Or don't. Just be good to him."

"Wild that you don't worry if he'll be good to me."

"He wants you to move in with him. He's moony-eyed and insane now. You've ruined him. From what I can tell, you're the same as ever."

"Except for the part where I'm not," he said.

"What's that supposed to mean?"

"Never mind. Nothing."

Devon ended the call before he could do something stupid like admit to her that he was truly considering Carl's suggestion of going to L.A. for a semester at least. The road trip across the country alone was a selling point. He'd always wanted to see New Orleans, and Roswell, and the Grand Canyon. He'd always wanted to drive Highway 1 along the coast. Something told him Carl would be open to all of that.

And open to his dick in every single motel room they

crashed in.

He wanted it. He wanted that so bad.

"C'mon," he said, handing his phone back to him. "Let's eat. And do some research."

"What kind of research?" Carl asked as he followed him down the stairs.

"Into roadside attractions on the way to California."

"Really?"

Devon smirked at the surprise and excitement in Carl's voice. "What? You didn't think you'd fucked me good enough to convince me to go?"

Carl drew up his usual seat at the kitchen counter. Devon threw open the cupboards and retrieved PB&J and bread. Hope's pot roast was ridiculous.

"That's not the only reason, though, right?" Carl asked. "I mean, I'm so into sex with you, don't get me wrong, and even if that's the only reason you're thinking about—"

"Carl?"

"Yeah?"

"You're hot, you're amazing in bed, you're surprising, and you're offering me the adventure of a lifetime. I'm twenty and I want to see what's out there. With you. I want to go."

"Wow, my dick really did a number on you," Carl said, coming around the counter and pressing his hand to Devon's forehead. "You're not feverish. So you must mean it."

Devon laughed, pulling Carl close to him. "It's a semester. Or a lifetime. I don't know. But you, me, this? Let's see what it looks like on a road trip at least."

"Yeah?"

"Yeah."

"Okay."

"Okay," Devon said, kissing Carl's mouth.

It was the purest kiss they'd ever shared. And it made his knees weak in a way that had nothing to do with sex and everything to do with a fresh shoot of something new growing in his heart.

SATURDAY

Chapter Eleven

"THAT'S AMAZING," CARL said, indicating the list of roadside attractions they'd found in Texas. "Put that on the list."

"And we can stay in this motel here," Devon said, indicating a roadside inn that promised clean sheets and little else.

"Hot sex in a cold town. I'm up for it," Carl whispered.

"Feeling horny again?" Devon asked as they put the finishing touches on that leg of the journey they'd been researching for the last several hours. They'd needed a break to get their second wind—or was this their tenth wind? Whatever the case, he was getting a little horny, too, thinking of Carl's little ass bent over some motel's bed, stuffed full with a toy that they'd have bought at the adult sex store several stops beforehand.

Jesus.

Devon was not going to miss out on the sex trip of a lifetime, even if the stay in L.A. turned out to be a bust. And he wasn't convinced that it would be. As he and

Carl had talked about the trip and explored potential stops and stopovers, he'd found they had the same sense of humor, the same interest in kitsch and culture, and the same taste in food. They'd even both said they liked to sleep in a cold room at night, and preferred romantic comedies to action flicks.

If nothing else, Devon thought the chances were good the two of them would come out of this as very good friends who'd had some amazing sex together. But he actually was starting to believe, as absurd as it was after only a few days, and most of that time spent spinning each other up to orgasm, that there was something real between them.

Or the seed of it anyway.

Carl had been right: he did know Devon well in his own way, and they did click. Now that Carl spoke to him, now that he wasn't hiding his vulnerability and stutter. Now that he'd shown Devon everything when he'd quivered and quaked on his dick.

Speaking of, Devon really wanted back inside Carl again.

Getting fucked had been unreal, amazing, earth-shattering, but he wanted Carl on the receiving end now. He wanted to hold him down and fuck him until he cried with pleasure, until he twitched and convulsed in orgasm, and until he said something he shouldn't in the heat of the moment.

Something like Devon had, but sweeter.

Could Devon fuck a confession of love out of Carl? He thought he could.

He just needed to lay the rail right, and Carl would spill over with a screaming confession, even if it was all pheromones and jizz talking. It'd still be fun to hear. And hot to bring about.

"My balls are a little eek," Carl said when Devon squeezed his thigh seductively. "Not sure what I want more—sex, or no more sex until tomorrow?"

Devon's dreams of being in Carl sputtered out. "Oh, man, yeah. Let's just watch TV, then." He got up to fetch a bottle of water. "C'mon. Let's hydrate. Both of us. And watch a show or two. Then we could go on a walk or something. Get away from the house."

"Yeah?" Carl sounded worried.

"There's time," Devon said. "We'll do it again. But it'll be more fun if you're rested, and your balls aren't angry-tired."

Carl laughed. "Chill out, balls," he said to his crotch. "Walk first, and then the TV and napping?"

"Yeah. Let's do it."

The weather was nice, but the road through the neighborhood was littered with leaves and pine needles from the storm that had rolled through.

"C'mon," Carl said, taking hold of Devon's hand. "Let's take the short cut to the trail."

Devon hesitated. The shortcut involved a little bit of trespassing, and while he and Hope had done it often enough as kids, now that he was grown, he was less enamored of the prospect. But if they didn't take the short cut, then they'd have to go over some big hills, and around the typically flooded area at the bottom to reach the walking trail they'd set out to enjoy.

"All right," Devon said when Carl squeezed his hand and lifted a challenging eyebrow. "But if Mr. Maddox calls my folks, I'm going to tell them it was your idea."

"And if your folks ask why you were hanging out with me what are you going to say?"

"That you seduced me and coerced me into a life of petty crime, but only after convincing me to drop out of school and pursue you across the country."

"Well, when you put it like that," Carl said, laughing, "it all sounds very deranged and kinda hot. Like I'm Clyde, and you're Bonnie."

"I'm Bonnie?" Devon huffed, letting Carl lead the way through Mr. Maddox's prized orchard, carved into the hillside with his neighbor's hard work and sweat of years—which was why he didn't like people tramping through it. "You're the pretty one."

Carl looked over his shoulder, a surprised smile on his lips. "You think I'm pretty?"

"You don't?"

"I do. I mean, I have a mirror. But I don't know, it's

nice to hear it from you."

"Anytime."

"You're pretty, too."

"Thanks, Bonnie."

Carl chuckled. "No, I'm Clyde, and you're Bonnie. I'm the cool musician. You're the tagalong."

"Oooh, low blow," Devon murmured. "I guess in that case we're more like Sid and Nancy. Let's hope we don't end up like them either, though."

"Who?"

"Old people. Dead people. Punk rock people. My dad made me watch some documentary about them because he used to think they were cool when he was young. They were like the Bonnie and Clyde of punk, I guess."

"We could be the Bonnie and Clyde of studio musicians or cruise ship guitarists," Carl said, laughing, as they approached the fence they'd have to leap in order to reach the cut-through to the trail. "Or the Sid and, who?"

"Nancy."

"Yeah," Carl said, hefting himself up and over the simple log rail fence, and reaching for Devon. "C'mon. Up and over."

"Devon Waters!" The bellow from the backside of the house next to the small orchard told them Mr. Maddox had woken from his mid-day nap, and they were caught. "I'm calling your mother!"

"Sorry, Mr. Maddox," Devon yelled as he leaped the fence. "Won't happen again!"

"It better not!" The old man appeared on his back porch and held up his cell phone. "I have her on speed dial because of your sister and her blond boyfriend!"

"Guess that's you," Devon said to Carl as he slunk away up the trail into the woods, avoiding Mr. Maddox's scolding. "Sorry again, Mr. Maddox! Last time! I swear!"

Mr. Maddox headed back inside, shaking his head, but Devon felt pretty sure he wasn't actually going to call his mother. But, if he did, then Devon would just apologize and make the same promise he'd just made: last time, never again, yadda.

"You're so cute," Carl said, coming back down the path toward Devon and taking his hand. "'Oh, please, Mr. Maddox, don't be mad!' Adorable."

"I didn't say that."

Carl went up on his tiptoes and pushed Devon's curls off his forehead. "You might as well have. God, you're gorgeous. In this light, and with your hair all curled up from the humidity out here. Stay there—" Carl pulled his phone out and held it up. "Just—there. Now it's captured forever. I can look back and remember this weekend."

"Look back from where?" Devon asked, suddenly worried that Carl might not be serious about the entire cross-country, adventure-in-L.A., possible cruise ship job yarns he'd been spinning.

"From our five-year anniversary," Carl said, laughing. "I don't know where I'll be looking back from, but it could just as easily be that as anything else, right?"

Devon shrugged. He knew this was all madness. Two days ago he hadn't even been sure he wanted to even have sex with Carl, and now he was seriously, *very* seriously, considering taking a sabbatical and trying out a whole new direction in life.

His mom was going to kill him. His dad would want to too, probably, but less so than his mom. She'd always told him that he was her reliable son, and she knew she could count on him to make good choices.

What he was doing with Carl this weekend, and this whole new wild future he now envisioned was anything but a good choice. But it was an exciting choice. And when was the last time he'd been this excited? He supposed when he first got to fuck Carl's sweet ass.

Which was—*God*—so incredibly fuckable, and tight, and hot, and…

Focus, Devon!

He frowned, following Carl up the path. It was all dappled with autumn light and littered with slick brown leaves and pine needles. Carl looked elfin, stepping through all the lushness of the woods with a light step. His hair glowed, and his skin did, too, and those white-blue eyes seemed almost magical as he traipsed onward into the forest.

"Up here," Carl said, motioning for Devon to keep up. "There's a nice spot. Hope and I come up here to smoke weed sometimes, but—" He shrugged. "I don't actually smoke it anymore. Always makes me paranoid."

"Yeah?"

Carl wrinkled his nose. "Yeah. Like I'd become convinced someone was spying on us up here. That sort of thing. It was too creepy. Hope swears we just need to get a different supplier with better stuff, but what's the point? If it's not fun for me, why bother. I mean, it's still illegal here after all. She loves it, though. Calms her brain down."

Devon could relate. Whenever he was overwhelmed between school and his O'Charley's schedule, he'd unwind with Xander, his coworker, behind the dumpsters after work was over. Then he'd walk back to his dorm, feeling pleasantly buzzed and relaxed. Ready to study and eat a bag of chips or three.

But it wasn't like he had to have it.

"We keep some supplies up here, though," Carl said, approaching a sizable fallen tree that was hollowed out inside, and the massive, nearly bench-shaped rock beside it. "Lighters, candles, gummy bears, that sort of thing."

"Gummy bears?" Devon said, watching as Carl knelt in the pine needles and peered into the log using his flashlight. "Checking for snakes or other ghoulies," he said before reaching inside and tugging out a Ziplock bag. Inside, sure enough, Devon could make out a package of gummy bears, a lighter, a few tea light candles, and what looked like a pack of cigarettes.

"Do you smoke?"

"Huh?" Carl glanced at the bag and grimaced. "Hope and I tried it. Thought it might look cool on stage, you know? But, ugh. I'd rather eat ass than smoke a cigarette." A sudden grin cracked over his face and his eyes lit up even brighter. "I guess I mean that literally now. I'd much rather eat ass. That only leads to orgasm, unlike cigarettes which lead to coughing, gagging, and smelling like, well, cigarettes, you know?"

Devon watched Carl take a seat on the big stone bench, and he climbed onto it, too. It was big enough that they could sit cross-legged facing each other.

"Okay," Carl said, pulling out the tea light candles, the lighter, the gummy bears, and a piece of chalk that Devon hadn't noticed before. "First we draw a pentagram, like this," he said.

And Devon watched, surprised, as Carl did draw a big pentagram between them. "What are you doing?"

"Magic," Carl offered, with a little grin. "Fairy magic."

Devon blinked at him.

"Kidding. But, yeah, sometimes I like to cast a spell

or two. It can be fun."

Devon shrugged, a nagging uncertainty in his gut, but he watched as Carl put a tea light on each point of the pentagram before lighting them.

"Now, we have to focus on what we want," Carl said.

"What we want?" Devon repeated.

"Like when I did this last week, I focused on you agreeing to this weekend, and look. It worked."

"You cast a spell on me?" Devon asked, trying to not feel a little weirded out by that. The forest around them smelled of wet dirt, disintegrating leaves, and fresh air, but the light that sparkled off the water droplets all around and filtered through the swaying tree tops did feel otherworldly. Plus, he was tired, so tired, and drained, and kinda horny still. He felt a little possessed, actually.

"J-just a l-li-li—ugh. A small one," Carl said, with a shrug. "Do you c-care?"

The stutter. He was anxious now.

Devon looked at the small, flickering candles and up into Carl's glittery eyes. He didn't care. If he was told that he was hypnotized into this weekend, he'd be happy about it. If he was told that he'd been put under a powerful elf's spell, he'd be glad. The time he'd spent with Carl was already the most interesting and arousing he'd ever had.

"No, I don't mind." Devon said. "How do we do a

spell?"

"First, like I ss-said, you f-focus on what you w-want."

So Carl was still nervous now, or vulnerable, or both. Devon closed his eyes. "I'm focusing on us, in the car, laughing, singing, fucking in motels, seeing the Grand Canyon, driving Highway 1, getting an apartment in LA, living there—"

"Cruise ship," Carl inserted.

"Getting a job on a cruise ship."

"All right," Carl said breathlessly. "Now we pull out some of our hair, and we burn it in the center candle."

"Burn our hair?"

"Mm-hmm." Carl was already pulling out multiple strands, so Devon did the same.

They both lit the ends of the strands and dropped them onto the rock, watching them go up quickly. Devon wrinkled his nose. The smell of burnt hair was kind of gross.

"Now we toast it with gummy bears," Carl said, getting out two bears, handing a green one to Devon and taking an orange for himself. "To all of that," he said, and they touched the bears together. "Now swallow it without chewing," he said, tossing the gummy bear into his mouth and gulping it down.

Devon did as commanded, and they sat for a long, quiet moment, listening to the wind in the trees.

"Good," Carl said, leaning over and blowing out the candles. "That should do it."

Devon laughed a little, but Carl shot him a serious look and he sucked it back, pulling a serious face.

After clearing away the supplies, except for the gummy bears, which he left out, Carl hopped down from their perch and stashed it all back inside the log. Then he got on the rock again, shifting so that he could lie with his head in Devon's lap.

"Hi," he said, gazing up at Devon.

Devon fingered his hair, noting the softness and the way it slipped through his fingers as he tugged. "Hi," he whispered.

They sat in silence for a long time, and it was comfortable, precious. Devon didn't feel the need to talk, and neither, it seemed, did Carl. Instead they compared hand sizes, touched fingers and forearms, and, eventually, sat facing each other while holding hands and staring into each other's eyes.

No words seemed to touch the intimacy of that experience. Only sex topped it, in Devon's opinion, and even then, who knew? This prolonged eye contact and slow breathing was like a drug. He'd almost believe those gummy bears were edibles, if he hadn't seen the Haribo packaging. He was flying high, dreamy and loose, and Carl was there with him.

The rain was the only reason they moved.

It started like a plucking melody on the leaves above, but soon it was a wild rush, and Devon wasn't about to walk out of the shelter of the forest and into it. Not yet, anyway.

Instead, he pulled Carl close, and the two of them ventured farther into the woods, a little off the trail, where Carl said he knew of a small overhang that they could wait out the weather.

"You really are an elf," Devon said as Carl tucked them back into a crevice of a rock wall at the side of the mountain. It was dry back there, almost like a cave, but still open at the top, aside from the overhang. "You know a lot about this mountain."

"Escaped from elf land to play music and seduce human men," Carl said teasingly. "That's me."

Devon tilted Carl's head up and thumbed his chin. "Can you be an elf in L.A.?"

Carl shrugged. "Since I'm not really an elf, it doesn't matter, does it?"

"Mm," Devon said, and he rubbed his nose against Carl's perfect one. "I could blow you here."

Carl's lips twitched up, and he leaned back against the rock wall and unbuckled his pants. "I could let you."

Devon dropped to his knees and spent the rest of the rainstorm with Carl's cock in his mouth. By the time the rain passed, his lips were bruised and aching, but he had the sweet taste of Carl's load on his tongue and the sound of Carl's ecstatic cry echoing in his ears.

He hoped whatever magic Carl had cast never came undone.

It was crazy, and it was wild, but Devon liked being under Carl Pink's spell.

Chapter Twelve

B ACK AT THE house, hot cocoa was in order, and then came a long sucking practice in front of the TV. For his part, Devon kept his eyes on the screen, trying to concentrate as various images passed by and storylines played out, but all he could really think about was the man at his feet, the mouth on his cock, and the long, agonizing *"practice"* Carl was indulging in.

"What's going on now?" Carl said, pulling off to wipe his mouth with the back of his hand and quizzing Devon about the show. It was a game he'd come up with on the way home. Devon had to watch, reporting to Carl what was happening while Carl worked on his cock-sucking skills. It was devastatingly difficult, and Devon was on the verge of just bullshitting an answer when his brain coughed up an explanation of some of the visuals he'd taken in while trying not to push his dick into Carl's throat.

"Um, Snow White is discovering that, uh, the long-haired girl is her daughter? But all grown? And, god-dammit, Carl, holy fuck," he whispered as his cock was engulfed in wet heat again. "I have to come soon."

But Carl just hummed and tried to take Devon in deeper. He wasn't trying to deep throat, but he was definitely working on reducing his gag reflex, and, so far, he was succeeding, taking Devon in past his soft palate and to the very top of his throat.

"Snow is crying," Devon squeezed out. "She's—fuck, fuck. Damn. Unf."

Carl pulled off again. "Why's she crying?"

"The baby…the baby…" He moaned as Carl worked his shaft. "I quit. You win."

"There's no winner like that," Carl said. "If you quit, then I quit. So just losers all around."

Devon gritted his teeth. "You love orgasm denial."

"It's my favorite thing to watch in porn," Carl agreed, putting out his tongue to lick the head of Devon's cock. "How about you?"

"I never cared one way or another before."

"Now?"

"Now I want to come, for fuck's sake."

Carl laughed, his eyes glittering. "Should have envisioned me letting you come when we cast that spell earlier today."

"Should never have punched your v-card if this is how you're going to be," Devon muttered as Carl swirled his tongue over and around his slit. "Should have left you unpunched."

"My magic's too strong," Carl whispered. "Plus you like it."

"I don't."

"You do," Carl argued. "Wait and see. You'll love it."

Devon's nipples ached and he plucked them while gazing at where Carl was spitting on his fingers, promising more.

"What's happening now?" Carl asked.

Devon flitted his gaze to the screen. "The episodes over. A new one is starting."

"Nice," Carl said. "I've kept you hard for forty-five minutes then."

Devon squirmed. "It's long enough."

"Mm-hm, I'll decide." Carl had slipped lower, and he tapped the spit-wet pads of his fingers against Devon's hole. "Bear down for me."

Carl had learned all too well the last few days, and now Devon was the one being told what to do, how to open up, and when he'd get to come. It was absurd, and yet here they were.

Devon moaned as Carl's finger slid into him, a little rough with only spit to lubricate, but then so fucking good as Carl pushed against his prostate. "Yessss," Devon slurred. "Fuck, yessss."

"I knew you liked it," Carl said, smugly.

Devon didn't answer, his eyes rolling up as Carl worked his prostate and went back to sucking his cock.

The game seemed to be over, though, because no more questions came his way about the show and what was happening on it, but the orgasm didn't seem to be any closer, either.

Devon's legs shook, and his stomach muscles jumped, but that final barrier to climax just couldn't be breached. He started to feel desperate and a little scared. He'd never been unable to come before. He'd never been so shot out that he was empty, or whatever was going on with him now.

"That's good," Carl cooed when he released his cock and sat back with his finger still jammed inside. "You're so hard."

Devon squirmed on Carl's finger and gritted out, "I can't come. I can't."

"Ah," Carl whispered. "I think you can."

Devon shook his head, tears pricking behind his closed lids. "I think I'm spent out. I'm too…I don't know. I can't."

Carl slipped his finger free. "Wait here, baby. I'll be back to help you."

Devon shivered and shook, feeling weird and scared, and also as if he were still flooded with that magic they'd touched in the forest. He waited, worried and horny, and strung out on too much sex, and too much new hope— and then Carl was back with lube and a condom.

"I'll fuck you," Carl said, kissing Devon's temple.

"That'll make you come for me, won't it?"

Devon nodded, though he didn't know for sure anymore. He might just stay caught here on this magical edge of bliss and pain, where he was aroused and needy, but couldn't reach completion, forever.

"You're okay," Carl said, sliding lubed fingers into Devon.

Devon shifted so his ass was at the edge of the sofa. He pulled Carl toward him, letting his sheathed cock breach him and slide home. It was a big stretch, just like last time, and Carl hit his prostate, just like last time. But unlike last time, the end didn't come quickly.

Devon was sweating and twisting, arching and aching, and it was only when he thought he'd never, *ever* come that he finally did. It punched into him like a lightning strike and wrenched him hard. He shouted, and he pumped a small load onto his stomach as Carl cooed and stroked his cock in time to his own pounding thrusts.

The moment expanded and held, and passed again, leaving him spent and wasted. Carl was still hard and moving, and Devon was a little overstimulated, but he wouldn't ask him to stop. Not until he'd come, too.

And when Carl did reach orgasm, it was beautiful. His elfin face twisted with pleasure, his magical eyes shone so bright, and his words were all for Devon: "Fuck, I love you, baby, this is so good, I love you."

Devon opened his mouth to say the same, but the words were punched away by Carl's last few thrusts, and all he gave was a small, exhausted gasp. They lay together, sweaty, and still needful, despite being drained.

SUNDAY

IT WAS A full twenty-four hours before their next orgasm.

But neither of them minded. They were far too wrapped up in their planning, and kissing, and cuddling. Their napping, and their hikes into the forest to cast more spells.

On the second trip, Carl took an index card with him, into which he'd punched a half-dozen holes. During the spell-casting, he'd burned the card, saying that his virginity was renewed, and would be forever, so long as he was only with Devon.

"Why?" Devon asked. "I thought you wanted to stop being a virgin?"

"Because I want to stay *your* virgin," Carl said. "Your bossy, demanding virgin." He grinned. "Besides, it just means you get to punch my v-card again and again."

"I'd do that anyway," Devon assured him.

"I know."

Chapter Thirteen

"So you've fucked him six ways to Sunday, I hear," Hope said into Devon's ear through the tinny cell phone connection.

He cringed. "Don't make it sound like that."

"I'm glad, I really am," she said, but she didn't entirely sound it. "I mean, I'm happy that you guys clicked and all, but do you think maybe you're going overboard with it all? Just a little?"

"Overboard? What's that mean?" Devon asked, thinking he must be stupid, because this sudden caution from Hope was something he hadn't seen coming. She'd been the one to set this up. She'd made them vegan pot roast!

"I mean, you're a great guy, and it was really sweet of you to take care of his pesky problem. It meant a lot to him because he's had a crush on you for so long. And don't get me wrong, I know how exciting Carl can be. He's been my best friend forever, and that's part of what's great about him. But you can't seriously be considering dropping out of school to go to Los Angeles with him?"

"Why not?"

She sighed, and Devon could just imagine her pinching the bridge of her nose between her fingers. "I just think you're letting this all go to your head. Traveling across the country with nothing? Starting fresh there with no job, no acceptance to a university? This isn't like you."

"What if it is now?"

"Devon, think logically. You don't have the same things to fall back on if this all goes wrong. Carl's an only child of wealthy parents, and you're…well, Mom and Dad can't afford to save you if you get out there and it doesn't work out."

Devon dragged his hand through his hair before peeking back through the patio door window to see that, yes, Carl was still asleep on the sofa. He'd fallen asleep while playing his guitar, and Devon had had to slip it from his hands, help lay Carl down, and place the guitar in a safe place across the room. He'd been so tired. Sex weekends were exhausting. No doubt about it. "Look, I hear what you're saying. I'm just—"

"Being kind to him. Helping him before he leaves. That was all you agreed to, and that's all you're supposed to be doing. Don't get carried away."

"I'm not getting carried away." Devon cleared his throat, embarrassment welling up at the lie, because of course he was getting carried away. He was swept off his feet. He was falling headfirst. He didn't want it to end. "Carl is so… It's just that he's… And well, I…" How did he explain this? He better figure it out, because talking with Hope about it was going to be so much easier than telling his parents. "He's amazing, and I think I could fall in love with him."

Hope let out a soft, sympathetic sound and heat rose in Devon's cheeks. Why was she making it out like he was being a fool? "Devon, please listen to yourself. You've never cared about Carl at all until this weekend. I had to beg you to do this for him, remember?"

"I was stupid."

"You were. But you don't have to continue that trend now."

"That's the thing! I want to continue this trend!" Doing what Carl wanted him to do was thrilling, exciting, wonderous. He didn't want to stop.

"I'm really worried that your dick has taken over for your brain."

"Maybe," Devon agreed. "But why not see if it knows what it's doing?"

"Because dicks never know what they're doing. Dicks are dumb."

"So caring about Carl is dumb?"

"Noooo," Hope moaned through the phone. "You're being so irritating. Of course not. But all this dreamy stuff about traveling across the country, and living together in L.A., and getting a job on a cruise ship, or whatever. I mean, I love Carl. Don't get me wrong. But he's a romantic. And that's just how he is. But you? You're not like him and never have been. You're just regular old Devon."

"Carl doesn't see me that way."

"That's because Carl's in love with you," Hope said with a huff of exasperation. "And he has been for, like, forever. But that doesn't mean you're in love with him, or that you're the right guy for him long term, *or* that you can just drop out of school and go to L.A. with him and say fuck real life."

"That could become my real life," Devon argued.

"No, because you're just Devon. He's Carl! He's Carl Fucking Pink, of Pinky and the One Eyes, and he's like some kind of, I don't know, magical gremlin or something. Everything, and I do mean *everything* always goes his way. But our lives aren't like that. Your life isn't."

"It is like that."

"What goes your way, Devon? Tell me."

"This? With him?"

"No, listen to me. I'm not trying to be mean, but think about it. Getting you to fuck him was, again, things going *his* way. Long-term, though, who's to say if you being in his life, being his boyfriend or whatever, is going to be what he wants."

"You said he's been in love with me for years, so he's not that changeable. Is he?" Devon hated that he even had to ask. A coldness fell over him. Hope did know Carl a lot better than he did.

"Changeable? Not really. But that's not the point. He's Carl, and you're…" She hesitated. "You're a normal human. A great guy, a wonderful brother, but just a typical human being."

"So is Carl! He isn't perfect. He stutters!"

"No kidding? I mean, that's not a secret. Do you have a problem with it?" Her tone had gone sharp with protectiveness.

"No! Of course not. Why would I?"

Silence reigned for a moment, before Hope spoke with a gentle kindness that burrowed into Devon's skin, into his heart. "He used to try to talk *me* into going with him, you know. It was going to be the two of us against the world. The two of us on a cruise ship. The two of us busking in France."

Devon swallowed around a new tightness in his throat. "You? Busking? You can't play an instrument."

"The flute, actually, if you recall."

"Two years in middle school band doesn't mean—"

She shushed him. "It doesn't matter. The thing is, I knew the whole time that Carl was the only one who was going to do those things. I just went along with it because it made him happy. But you? Do you really think you can live at his level. Honestly? Because you're putting your entire future on the line here betting that you can."

"Why couldn't I?"

"You're Devon Waters, and that's a pretty great guy to be. I love Devon Waters; most people would. But Carl's special in a way that you and I will never be."

Devon blinked at the sky. Rain was coming in again. The clouds were thick and dark. His stomach twisted weirdly. "Carl thinks I'm special too."

"I know this is crass, but it has to be said: Carl thinks you make him come his brains out. He's in your thrall right now, and I get it. What you've shared has been sweet and a dream come true for him. But other guys could do that for him too."

"I don't know about that."

"He's just lost his virginity to you, of course he doesn't want this to end. But, Devon, let's be serious. What are you going to do for him out there?"

"I don't get it. Are you saying he'll meet other guys out there and lose interest in me?"

"Maybe. Or maybe he'll be so worried about making things work with you that he won't fly as high as he otherwise might. You don't want to be the guy who brings him down or keeps him from reaching his potential. You don't want him to reject amazing opportunities that might not include you."

"You're such a bitch," Devon whispered, his throat tight. He felt guilty as soon as he said it.

"I know you think so now, but I just want the best for you and for Carl. This is hard to hear, but one day you'll thank me for being so honest with you."

"I won't," Devon said tightly. "Because I'm going with him. I'm sorry if you think that's short-sighted. But I'm not sorry that I feel alive and want to see what the future holds, and that just being with him for a few days has opened new horizons for me. I'm not sorry about that. And I'm not sorry that *I* have the guts you didn't have."

Hope was silent for a long time. Devon held his tongue, too. His stomach was jumpy, and he felt weird.

"That's all we have to say about this, then, I guess." Hope's voice was sad, and even though she'd been the one to say the most hurtful things, Devon felt guilty again.

Rain drops hit Devon's head, and he lifted his face so that they splashed onto his cheeks, too. "I guess so."

"See you soon, Devon. I love you."

"I know you do."

And he did know it, but it didn't mean what Hope had told him didn't hurt. He rubbed a hand over his chest and peered up at the gray sky.

Chapter Fourteen

"**H**OPE SAYS I shouldn't go with you," Devon said as he and Carl made dinner.

They were both starting to feel up to another round, and the end of the weekend was staring them in the face. If they were really going to do this thing, then sometime this evening Devon had to go back to his college campus to prepare for the next week. After that, he'd need to finish his semester, arrange for a sabbatical, and do a bunch of other stuff, too, like buy stuff for California, and get his car fixed up. They'd be taking it instead of Carl's stupid but cool Camaro.

"I know."

"She thinks I'm being a dick-struck idiot."

"She said that?"

"No. She said that we're both getting carried away."

"That sounds more like her."

"She also says you're special and the world is your oyster."

"Mm-hmm."

"She says I'm not special enough for you and, in the

end, I'll just drag you down."

Carl's eyes snapped up from the PB&J he was making and he dropped his knife to step to Devon's side. "You? Not special? *You?*"

Devon shrugged. "I mean, she's not wrong. I'm just an average student, and I work at O'Charleys, you know? I don't have any real dreams or aspirations or—"

"Get on your knees," Carl said.

"What?"

"On your knees. Now."

Devon blinked, put the jam jar he was holding on the counter, swallowed hard, and knelt at Carl's feet. He closed his eyes and waited.

Carl's fingers combed into his hair. "There. That's where you belong."

"What?" Devon asked, nearly choking on his own spit.

"You belong with me. At my feet. Doing what I say. Following me, supporting me, adventuring with me, casting spells with me, and fucking me. Tell me you disagree."

Devon shook his head. He couldn't deny it. He loved everything about being under Carl's command, and even though he was older, and more experienced, and supposedly steadier, he loved when Carl led him in whatever they were doing.

"Good."

Devon looked up, and Carl smiled at him, sliding his fingers over Devon's cheeks.

"Hope can't understand this," Carl said. "She won't get it. There's no reason to try to make her see. It's like white noise to her, right? Just something that filters right on out. How can she see that you're special like this when it's a part of you she can't ever know?"

Devon swallowed hard. "This makes me special to you?"

"Of course." Carl stroked his cheekbone again. "Plus, have you seen your face?"

Devon huffed a laugh.

"So handsome. And your mouth—" Carl rubbed his thumb along Devon's bottom lip. "Open it."

Devon frowned but did as he was told and Carl pushed his thumb inside, touching his tongue, and then pulled his thumb out again. "Now, put your tongue out."

Devon did and watched as Carl unbuttoned his jeans and took out his cock. It wasn't entirely hard, but he stroked it a few times, gazing at Devon as it grew into its full, thick hardness. He put the head of it against the flat of Devon's tongue and held it there.

"Focus," he said. "I'm going to cast a spell."

Devon held his tongue in place and watched as Carl stroked his own cock and spoke, slowly, evenly, and without a hint of a stutter. "You and me. In a car.

Laughing. Singing. You and me. In a motel. On the bed. You licking my asshole. Me sucking your cock. You and me in L.A.. Eating ice cream. You and me. You at my feet. You and me. You and me. You and me." Carl put his head back, and a little pulse of pre-cum fell onto Devon's tongue.

"Eat it," Carl said, pulling back, and releasing his cock, letting it stick out—red and gorgeous—from his body while Devon closed his mouth around the pre-cum and swallowed it. "Good boy."

He helped Devon up to standing. "Hope will get used to being wrong about this. Don't worry. I'll talk to her, too," he muttered fiercely. "By tomorrow night she'll be begging you for forgiveness."

"You don't need to talk to her. She's my sister and she wasn't trying to be mean. She just wanted to protect me—well, protect us both."

"I know. But she's my best friend, and I'm going to tell her what I think of the way she underestimates my boyfriend. But in the end, it won't matter if what she thinks of you coming to L.A. with me. The spell is cast. The future is us. Together."

"Do you really believe in magic?" Devon asked.

Carl shrugged, "I believe in all I just said, don't you?"

"I want to."

"Then trust it. Don't let Hope get under your skin or into your head."

"You're just afraid I'll back out of our plan."

Carl smiled. "Maybe a little."

"I won't," Devon said.

He didn't know how to explain to Carl that this weekend had been the best thing to happen to him, that he was grateful beyond words for what he'd experienced, and the new future ahead of them. So instead he said, "When I get to the dorm tonight, I'll text you when I arrive."

"Yes," Carl agreed. "And I'll text back."

Devon laughed. "Why would you say that?"

"Just in case you were worried I wouldn't."

"You're weird."

"I know."

The kiss touched Devon down to his core, and he wasn't at all surprised when dinner was abandoned, and Carl led him back upstairs. There was only a little time left now before their weekend would have to end, and neither one of them wanted to let go of the other.

Chapter Fifteen

CARL

FEELING SKIN ON skin was the best, Carl decided, and he looked forward to the day when he and Devon could be together without a condom, too. Soon, he knew. Devon was going to get a checkup from student health, so the next time they saw each other—which might be sooner than Devon was expecting, because Carl did have a car and did *not* have classes, a job, or any responsibilities beyond planning his move to L.A.—they could be together bare.

But, for now, he was curled up on his side with Devon fucking into him from behind, his entire back touching Devon's front. He felt safe and protected, and open and vulnerable. He loved the sensations and the beautiful bubble they created over the long weekend in Devon's bed. This time, it was tender, and slow, and at the rate they were going, it was going to be ages before he came. But he liked waiting almost as much as he liked making Devon wait.

This "deflowering" hadn't gone the way Carl had

imagined it would.

No, it'd gone even *better*.

When he'd cast his spell with Hope last week before they'd managed to get Devon on board with the plan, he hadn't let himself picture anything beyond getting Devon naked and inside him. But now? Now his dreams were expanding moment by precious moment.

With each stroke of Devon's cock, he imagined a bigger future. Not just him alone in a new city, but Devon by his side. Devon's smile slicing him open with its sweetness when they found the perfect apartment. Devon waiting for him outside a studio where he'd just laid down tracks for a band. Devon applying for jobs with him. Devon high-fiving him when they both scored the cruise ship gig—because he *did* want to see the world. With Devon there beside him to take it all in. To help him hold it all. To make it real.

And he wanted to be the one to give everything to Devon, to inspire him to reach for each new experience and help lead him through it. Like he was giving Devon his ass right now, and inspiring him to chase his pleasure, and leading him to another shattering orgasm. Carl had never known before how sex could be so analogous to so many things, how it could echo life so thoroughly. The frustration, the action, the pleasure, the desperation, the climax, the aftermath…

It was like playing the guitar: crushing it through the

chorus and bridge before bringing it down for a gentle landing. It was like casting a spell: the set-up, the focus, the intensity, the hope, then the clean-up. It was like traveling cross-country: the anticipation, the excitement-laced movement, the false stops and starts, the destination that felt too far and yet too close, and the arrival at a new home. It was like falling in love with Devon: first seeing him, watching him, wanting him, yearning, reaching, pining, aching, and finally, finally having him—as heady as orgasm, as satisfying as the after bliss.

Devon had agreed to teach Carl about sex, but he'd taught him about life. There would always be a post-fuck drop. The crash. The ending. But, if you were lucky, there would always be a new beginning, too. A few hours later when the refraction period ended. Every effort required rest in order to continue. Truly, sex was full of life lessons.

Devon's mouth roamed over the back of Carl's neck, leaving wet, tingling sensation it its wake. Devon sucked on his earlobe, making him shiver all over. "Ready to take more?" he asked, his voice throaty.

"No," Carl said, almost laughing at the surprised stutter in Devon's hips. "Stay slow. We're going to make this one last."

Devon groaned and slipped a hand up from where he'd been gripping Carl's hips to rub at his nipples. "What about this?"

"Do it," Carl agreed.

Devon's fingers worked Carl's nipples in time to his thrusts, and his eyes rolled back, his hips stilling as he took Devon's steady rhythm. His cock leaked drops of pre-cum as it strained for more attention.

Carl was fair, though. If he was going to deny Devon, he was going to deny himself, too, so he didn't take his cock in hand, instead just reveling in the slide and friction of being fucked and the pinching pleasure at his nipples.

"You're gonna be the death of me," Devon muttered into Carl's damp hair. "I'm gonna go with you out west and you're going to fuck me into thin air."

"Mm, that's a dangerous magic," Carl said. "But it wouldn't serve my purposes. I need you solid, and hard"—he squeezed around Devon's cock for emphasis—"to meet my needs."

Devon laughed. "I Googled while you napped."

"Googled what?" Carl asked breathlessly.

"How long the high of new love lasts."

"'Love'?" Carl reached back to hold Devon's hips as they moved, his cock flexing again and another pearl of pre-cum welling up. "Did you say love?"

"Mm, maybe, but I felt cheap Googling about infatuation."

Carl giggled and Devon moaned behind him.

"Feels good when you squeeze me like that," Devon

whispered. "Laugh again."

"Be funny again."

"I can't," Devon said. "I'm too deep into the euphoric stage."

"Mm?"

"The stage where you're like this. Non-stop fucking, arousal all the time, obsessively thinking of the other person, wanting to be together, optimistic, making choices like—moving across the country together, breathless, horny…" he groaned again, his hips thrusting faster. "Ung, the so-good phase. This. We're in it."

"It passes?"

"Yes," Devon said. "Or it calms. Yeah, calms."

"Do you want to be calm?" Carl said, working his asshole so that it gripped with each slow drag out. He grinned when Devon's breathing stuttered.

"No," he gasped.

"Good." They fucked languidly for a while, moaning and shuddering, but climax eluded them, which was exactly how Carl wanted it. As the lube grew tacky, Devon added more, and the unhurried ride continued.

"Why'd you Google?" Carl asked when Devon was huffing and seemed to be getting closer to orgasm again.

"Just need to know what to expect," Devon whimpered. "For us. When we aren't fucking like bunnies. When we are actually in L.A. together for real."

"Mm."

"What'd it say?"

"Said it could go either way. Said the crisis could lead to a break-up."

"S-so we're a couple," Carl said, bearing down to let Devon slide in deep. "We're t-together."

Devon breathed against Carl's neck, then whispered, "We are. I'm falling for you. You know that."

"I w-want you to say it."

"Say what?"

"Ask me to be your boyfriend." Carl squeezed around the thick base of Devon's cock. He felt Devon shudder against his back. "Ask me. Now."

"Carl, will you—" Devon pulled out and then thrust in. "Be my." He did it again. "Boyfriend?"

Carl twisted so he could kiss Devon's chin, and whispered, "Yes."

Devon gripped Carl's hips hard, and said, "Fuck, let me come."

Carl giggled. "Not yet."

"When?"

"After you tell me what it feels like to be inside me."

Devon hitched a breath. "Hot. Tight. Slick. Alive."

"And?"

"Beautiful. Fucking good. Need more. Always more."

"And?"

"And my heart feels soft."

"Your heart?"

"Yeah."

"Tell me."

"I did!" Devon nearly wailed. "Let me come, please!"

"Tell me how I make you feel. Inside." Carl chuckled. His own cock ached like a demon, and his balls were tight and hard, and each stroke over his prostate was a zap of joy, but he wanted to make Devon work for it. "Tell me."

"You make me feel crazy," Devon said. "And like I can do anything. Like fucking you is… God, Carl, you're so weird."

"Tell me."

"Like fucking you is the gate to my future. When I'm in you, anything is possible."

"Mmm," Carl moaned. "That's the hottest thing I've ever heard."

"You're the hottest thing in the world."

"Yeah?"

"Carl, please."

"Yes, let's come, baby. Make me come, and then you. Me first. Hurry."

Devon's thrusts grew frantic, and he reached around for Carl's cock. It was soon evident that Devon was too far gone to really get Carl off, as he struggled to both reach orgasm, and keep it at bay long enough for Carl to come. "Help," Devon muttered. "Help me?"

Carl took hold of his own cock, placing his hand on top of Devon's, and together they were able to reach a pace that had Carl tensing, flexing, reaching—

Shattering.

His cum flew over the sheets, and his asshole convulsed on Devon's plunging cock. He shouted, his vision whiting out, juddering with pleasure that was both too long and too short.

Carl came back to his senses as Devon broke apart behind him. The shout of pleasure and the hunching of his body dissolved into tremors as his cock pulsed hard against the rim of Carl's hole.

"That's it," Carl muttered. "Good boy, Devon. You're my good boy."

Devon moaned and rubbed his face in Carl's hair, his hands flexing on Carl's hips, and his sweaty body still straining into him.

Carl smiled.

This was heaven. This was a new beginning. This was magic beyond his understanding. This was more than punching his v-card, this was the start of an endless, vast future for them both. He couldn't even begin to see the end to it. It was just forever and onward. Adventure and growth, and new experiences, and love.

Yes, love. Devon hadn't been wrong to Google it.

Carl groaned as Devon dislodged his still swollen cock from Carl's ass. He watched languidly as Devon tossed the condom into the bedside trash.

"I love you," Carl said as Devon turned back to him and curled up on Carl's chest. He was bigger, but he fit so perfectly, in Carl's opinion. "I really do. I love you."

Devon kissed Carl's nipple and then his collarbone. "God, I know it's crazy, but I love you too."

Carl grinned, satisfaction seeping into every muscle, including his heart. He was at peace and right where he wanted to be.

Losing his virginity had felt so urgent, and now he knew why.

Devon was right. He'd said it first.

Losing his virginity had turned out to be the gateway to his future.

No, their future. Together.

Epilogue

DEVON

"Y**OU'VE GOT EVERYTHING?**" Hope asked, looking worried as she stood to the side, observing the final shove of luggage into the back of the Taurus. "You didn't forget the box from your bedroom?"

"Nope. Got it all," Devon said, watching his sister fret.

"You know I really am sorry if I was unkind that day." She met his gaze with dark, worried eyes. "I was feeling protective of you both. And maybe a little jealous."

"I know. I'm not mad at you."

It'd become obvious over the last two and a half months that Hope both supported their new relationship as she saw them together, and also mildly struggled with Carl being Devon's boyfriend now and not just her best friend.

Christmas Day, for example, she'd cooed over the exchange of gifts between Devon and Carl in front of the Christmas tree and clapped at the way their parents had made them pose for photos together as a couple. But she didn't love how their mom had started to call Carl "Devon's Carl" when referring to him amongst friends and family. That seemed to sting her in a way that Devon understood. After all, Carl had been *her* Carl for years.

But, in the end, she seemed to have made peace with her reservations about Devon embracing Carl's adventurous lifestyle, and with her shifting place in Carl's life.

The night before last, she'd come into Devon's bedroom and sat at the edge of his bed, picking at the comforter before saying, "I know I argued that you shouldn't go, that it was a bad idea and all that, but now I'm glad you are. This way, you'll be out there to keep him safe and take care of him."

"We can take care of each other," Devon had corrected.

"Yeah, you need taking care of too," she'd said with a teasing smile. "Carl says you do."

Devon had winced, wondering just what Carl had shared with her about the dynamic between the two of them, but Hope had dropped the teasing, saying instead, "I love you both, and I love that you love each other. Just know that if you ever need or want to come home, I'll drive across the country to get you."

"That's quite a promise."

"You know how I hate travel."

Devon had smiled. "I love you, Hope. But you won't have to make that long drive. I promise."

Hope had rolled her eyes, stood, and said, "I know I won't."

"Do you?" Devon had asked, surprised at her new faith.

"Yeah. He loves you. He's always loved you. And I can see that you've got it just as bad for him."

"I do."

Now the three of them stood by the Taurus saying their final goodbyes. Devon's parents had given them a farewell dinner two nights ago on their way out of town for work again. Carl's parents had blubbered over their boy the night before, alone, and had come with Carl to drop him off, leaving behind coffee in a thermos for their drive and a lipstick stain on Carl's cheek.

Hope, however, lingered on.

"Drive carefully," she said. "Don't get any tickets. Don't tailgate, and don't—"

"We know how to drive," Carl interrupted. "L-let's n-not m-m-m—argh! Don't make a big deal about it."

The frustration behind his stutter told Devon that Carl was feeling something big about leaving Hope behind. They'd been so close all through high school and after. The last few months had been fraught between them, too. He decided to leave them alone for a couple of minutes.

"I'm going to make one last sweep of my room and make sure I didn't forget anything," Devon said.

"Sure," Carl agreed and started toward the house, but Hope held his coat sleeve and Carl stayed behind.

Inside the house, Devon didn't bother with a final review of his room. He'd spent his holidays after the semester ended doing three things: explaining over and over to his parents why he was moving to L.A. and how he hadn't lost his mind, packing and re-packing and re-re-packing, and finding time to sneak off to be with Carl—sometimes in the woods to cast spells, or to "cast spells" beneath the rock overhang, and sometimes in Carl's bedroom to cast an even deeper, longer spell. He was certain he had everything he needed packed into the Taurus.

Instead, he stood by the window, peering out at the driveway as Hope and Carl talked. Hope dashed tears from her cheeks. Carl took her into a hug. They clung to each other, and Hope was the one to let go first.

Devon took a big breath and stepped back outside again. "Nope! I've got it all!" he called out.

"Time to go!" Carl said, glancing at his phone. "We're late already."

Devon grinned. He knew they were in no real rush. They'd planned their first stop only four hours away, so they could get into a motel room and get their clothes off. They hadn't been alone for any extended period since their first weekend, and neither thought they could handle an eight-hour drive before coming together. In each other. Bare.

For the first time.

Fuck.

Devon really wanted to get on the road and do just that. They should have just booked a hotel in town or something because he didn't want to wait.

Though he knew Carl loved to make him suffer.

And it had been Carl's idea to drive four hours the first day before stopping.

Final hugs were exchanged, and they climbed into Devon's car.

"Are y-you sure about th-this?" Carl asked from the passenger seat. "L-last chance to b-bail on me."

Devon took hold of his hand, kissed each knuckle, and started the car. "You couldn't get rid of me now if you tried."

Carl put on his seat belt with a smug expression. Waved one last time to Hope, then sighed with deep contentment. "I love you."

No stutter. No worry in his voice.

"I love you, too."

As they started down the driveway, the sun was shining and not a cloud was in the sky. Devon remembered two months earlier, driving the opposite way, the rain pouring in sheets, and the Camaro sitting in his garage.

The anticipation, the confusion, the revelation, the orgasm, the pleasure, the joy, and, best of all, the fall into sudden, life-changing love.

Punching Carl's v-card had been the best decision he'd ever made.

THE END

Join my newsletter to read the hot details of Carl and Devon's first time bare!

dl.bookfunnel.com/s9gx8830s6

one has ever made him feel so valuable and adored. Worthy. Strong.

No one has ever taught Matty how to fly. Or how to lose.

Rob might be a cowboy and a single dad who knows nothing about figure skating, but after only a few months, he's trained a new kind of bravery into Matty's soul.

But to achieve his Olympic dream, Matty will have to face the ultimate test. Has he truly learned what it means to win—on and off the ice—during his training season?

Training Season is a MM romance with a feisty, flamboyant figure skater and an easy-going dominant cowboy, opposites attract, hurt-comfort, single dad, winter holiday highlights, love beyond reason, multiple steamy scenes, and a well-earned happy ending. *This book contains some BDSM elements.*

Full-length

Younger Dom/Older sub

MR. NAUGHTY LIST
by Leta Blake

**A cute teacher gets a spanking this Christmas.
How hot can it get being on his former student's
Naughty List?**

Is Aaron allowed to want a hot holiday fling with his young former student? Even more forbidden, is he allowed to want this student to spank him?

It's another Christmas, and Aaron is still in the closet as a gay man and a natural submissive. With one youthful indiscretion blacking his ethics record, he can't afford to indulge his desires no matter how pent up and needy that leaves him.

Until his former student comes home for the holidays.

Dominant and charming, RJ knows what Aaron needs—intense, steamy encounters and a firm hand. As Christmas nears, RJ helps Aaron unlock his true self. But family and fallout await, and all good things must end.

Or can their hot holiday affair turn them into lasting lovers?

Mr. Naughty List is a steamy Christmas MM romance set in the *Home for the Holidays* series that began with *Mr. Frosty Pants*, but **can be read as a standalone**. Featuring light D/s, spanking, an older sub with a younger Dom, former student/teacher dynamics, and, of course, warm, sweet holiday feels complete with a strong happy ending.

Letter from Leta

Dear Reader,

Thank you so much for reading *Punching the V-Card*! It was a joy to write this sexy, light erotic romance for my readers, and I love Devon and Carl's cute, hot story. I hope you enjoyed reading it too!

I'd like to express my thanks again to Daniela and Gwen for beta reading and discussing their experience with stuttering with me. This novella is better for your input!

Be sure to follow me on BookBub or Goodreads to be notified of new releases. And look for me on Facebook for snippets of the day-to-day writing life, or join my Facebook Group for announcements and special giveaways. To see some sources of my inspiration, you can follow my Pinterest boards or Instagram.

If you enjoyed the novella, please take a moment to leave a review! Reviews not only help readers determine if a book is for them, but also help a book show up in site searches.

Also, for the audiobook connoisseurs out there, check for my books on Audible!

Thank you so much for being a reader!
Leta

Gay Romance Newsletter

Leta's newsletter will keep you up to date on her latest releases and news from the world of M/M romance. Join the mailing list today.

Leta Blake on Patreon

Become part of Leta Blake's Patreon community in order to access exclusive content, deleted scenes, extras, bonus stories, rewards, prizes, interviews, and more. www.patreon.com/letablake

Other Books by Leta Blake

Only You

Winter Holidays

North's Pole

The Mr. Christmas Series
Mr. Frosty Pants
Mr. Naughty List
Mr. Jingle Bells

A Boy for All Seasons
My December Daddy

Fantasy

Any Given Lifetime

Reimagined Fairy Tales

Flight
Levity

Paranormal & Shifters

Angel Undone
Omega Mine

Horror

Raise Up Heart

Heat of Love Series
White Heat
Slow Heat
Alpha Heat
Slow Birth
Bitter Heat

For Sale Series
Heat for Sale
Bully for Sale

Audiobooks
letablake.com/audiobooks

Discover more about the author online

Leta Blake
letablake.com

About the Author

Author of the bestselling book *Smoky Mountain Dreams* and fan favorites like *Training Season*, *Will & Patrick Wake Up Married*, and *Slow Heat*, Leta Blake has been captivating M/M Romance readers for over a decade. Whether writing contemporary romance or fantasy, she puts her psychology background to use creating complex characters and love stories that feel real. At home in the Southern U.S., Leta works hard at achieving balance between her writing and her family life.

www.ingramcontent.com/pod-product-compliance
Lightning Source LLC
Chambersburg PA
CBHW061537310726
48972CB00008B/2500